They traversed the trail to the memorial for Jessica's sister.

The same eerie feeling permeated the air, even with Finn on the trail behind her. The forest seemed to be holding its breath, the critters silent and watchful.

She rubbed the goose bumps on her arms.

"Let's make this quick." He flung an arm out toward the pile of teddy bears and flowers.

"The stuff looks like it's been moved around since this afternoon." Jessica ran her tongue around her dry mouth.

She glimpsed a black button eye from the depths of the pile, and her hands froze. With trembling fingers, she nudged aside the stuffed animals and candles to reveal the doll, staring at her from the center of the heap with its single eye.

Falling back in the dirt, she let out a piercing cry.

"What's wrong?" Finn swung around.

"That doll." She pointed a finger at the dirty rag doll with the yellow braids and red-checked blouse. "That's my doll from my childhood."

THE CREEKSIDE MURDER

CAROL ERICSON

H Harlequin

INTRIGUE

Harlequin® INTRIGUE™

Recycling programs for this product may not exist in your area.

ISBN-13: 978-1-335-45742-4

The Creekside Murder

Copyright © 2025 by Carol Ericson

 Harlequin Enterprises ULC
22 Adelaide St. West, 41st Floor
Toronto, Ontario M5H 4E3, Canada
www.Harlequin.com

Printed in Lithuania

MIX
Paper | Supporting responsible forestry
FSC® C021394

Carol Ericson is a bestselling, award-winning author of more than forty books. She has an eerie fascination for true-crime stories, a love of film noir and a weakness for reality TV, all of which fuel her imagination to create her own tales of murder, mayhem and mystery. To find out more about Carol and her current projects, please visit her website at www.carolericson.com, "where romance flirts with danger."

Visit the Author Profile page at Harlequin.com.

CAST OF CHARACTERS

Finn Karlsson—A Kitsap College professor and former sheriff's deputy, he's writing a true-crime book about the imprisoned Creekside Killer, but now another killer is on the loose, and the crimes are bringing up past memories and past heartaches.

Jessica Eller—A forensics analyst who refuses to believe her sister was murdered by the Creekside Killer ten years ago. When bodies start turning up, she's convinced that her sister's killer has resurfaced, and she's determined to unmask him this time, even if it puts a target on her back.

Avery Plank—Tagged the "Creekside Killer," this imprisoned murderer confessed to killing Jessica's sister, but he likes to play games.

Ashley King—Tiffany's best friend claims she doesn't remember anything unusual about the time her friend was murdered, but she knows more than she's admitting, and that knowledge could get her killed.

Denny Phelps—Tiffany's boyfriend at the time of her murder, now dating Ashley, was a drug dealer with some unsavory associates. Did one of them kill Tiffany, or did she know too much about Denny's business?

Dermott Webb—One of Finn's criminal justice students is a true-crime fanboy with an unusual appetite for serial killers.

Deke Macy—A campus employee with an unsavory interest in female college students, he knows all the murder victims and worked with Tiffany ten years ago. Have his cravings resurfaced?

Chapter One

Jessica had followed the trail to Tiffany's dead body hundreds of times in her mind. She hadn't expected the area to look so different now. She dug her hiking boots into the mushy ground to survey her position. The forest seemed to close in on her, suffocating her, warning her. She was done heeding warnings.

Huffing out a breath, she plowed ahead. She pushed aside the bushy shrub in front of her, tripping over its twisted trunk. She grabbed a handful of leaves to steady herself, their sharp edges scratching her palm. As she glanced down at the red lines crisscrossing her skin, she noticed the mulch of the forest floor giving way to dirt and pebbles.

She closed her eyes and cocked her head. Barely discernible beneath the whoosh of the breeze through the trees and the chattering birds, she detected the sound of gurgling water. Her lids flew open as her legs propelled her forward, her boots crunching over the gritty path that would take her to the water's edge—the place where a killer had dumped her sister's lifeless form ten years ago.

She broke through the trees a few feet before a babbling creek scurried over slick rocks and detoured around branches clawing their way out of the water—one shaped like an arm positioned to drag unsuspecting hikers into the water. Panting, she dropped to her knees and trailed her fingers in the icy stream until her fingertips turned white with the cold.

Her head dipped to her chest and the tears that had blurred her vision, threatening to overcome her on the trail, rolled down her cheeks and slid from her chin into the swirling water. The current carried them away but couldn't rid her of the pain lodged in her heart. She'd cried in this spot before…cried and raged and pounded the earth over the loss of her older sister, the sister who'd protected her in foster care.

They'd had different fathers—losers who'd abandoned Tammy, their mother, and them, without a backward glance or a penny for support. Tammy hardly batted an eye when they'd left. She just moved on to the next bum, who left her with a baby boy months before Tammy's death from an overdose.

When Tammy died, none of her family was interested in taking in her hodgepodge of kids, so they all went to foster care…except their brother. Just a baby, he'd been snapped up by some childless couple, eager to give him a great life.

He'd been the lucky one.

But Jessica'd been lucky to have Tiffany as her sister— until someone ended Tiffany's life. Jessica's gut told her that Tiffany's killer still roamed free and clear, but law enforcement disagreed.

Avery Plank sat in the Washington State Penitentiary for murdering a dozen women, including Tiffany. Although he'd never been convicted of her sister's murder, he'd confessed—adding it to his résumé while the cops closed the case and moved on. But Jessica refused to move on.

Now Morgan Flemming wouldn't let her move on.

The bushes rustled behind her, and Jessica twisted her body around to eye the tree line, the pebbles on the ground digging into her knees. She peered at the shivering branches and held her breath as a few birds winged it skyward.

She let it out on one word. "Hello?"

Her voice sounded small amid the unrelenting nature that pressed her on all sides. She cleared her throat and pushed to her feet, tugging on her down vest. "Anyone there?"

A twig snapped. Her heart pounded. She clapped a hand against the slick material covering her chest and licked her lips as her gaze darted back and forth across the wall of green.

Several seconds of silence later, she emitted a puff of air from her lips. Creatures big and small ruled the forest and typically stayed out of sight, especially during the daytime hours. She had nothing to fear from the animal variety. The human species was a different matter.

She yanked a couple of flowers from the red dogwood blooming creek side and tossed them into the water. She blew a kiss as the petals drifted away on the current.

Shoving her hands in the pockets of her vest, she tromped downstream, her boots leaving divots in the moist earth. She didn't have far to walk, and the creek led to her next destination.

Fifteen minutes later, she stumbled to a stop. A dirty piece of yellow tape fluttered from the end of a branch jutting into her path. She grabbed it and twirled it around her fisted hand as she scanned the memorial—a heap of teddy bears, bouquets of flowers, green felt pennants printed with the university's name, gutted candles, and cards, soaked through with moisture, the sentiments printed inside blurry and forgotten.

The outpouring for Tiffany hadn't been quite so effusive. After all, Tiffany hadn't been a student at the university. She'd worked in the cafeteria, a recovering junkie and sex worker...at least according to the police, but Jessica knew better. Her sister suffered from addictions, but she'd never been a sex worker.

Jessica sighed and released the yellow tape. It unraveled from her hand, leaving striped indentations. She ducked under another branch and picked her way over the pebbled shore to the shrine that had grown on the spot where a pair of hikers had discovered Morgan Flemming's body.

She crouched down and ran a finger over the head of a purple teddy bear, dislodging the crusted dirt from its fur. She chucked a couple bunches of motley flowers into the flowing water and righted a few candles. Most of the cards could be tossed, but maybe someone was saving them for the family. Whether the words could be read didn't really matter. The thought counted.

She stacked the cards and placed a candle on top of the pile. As she reached for the final card, it flipped open and the black scrawl inside caught her eye. Likely a newer card or protected from the elements by another offering, its letters weren't smudged.

As she flattened the card on her knee, her gaze skimming the words, icy fingers squeezed the back of her neck.

PROFESSOR FINN KARLSSON entered the last grade on his laptop and snapped the lid closed. He grabbed his briefcase and coffee and locked the door to his office behind him.

He had less than two minutes to make it to class, but dread slowed his pace, filling his shoes with lead.

He didn't want to spend another class discussing the murder of Morgan Flemming, but his criminal justice students hadn't wanted to talk about anything else since her body was discovered by the side of the creek a few weeks ago. He'd planned to introduce a new unit today, and he didn't want his students to sidetrack him again. Finn didn't have time to spend on the Morgan Flemming case. He had a prescribed amount of material to cover in a limited amount of time for the semester—at least that's what he told himself.

A minute later, as he walked through the side door of the lecture hall, he glanced at the seats full of eager students. This would've been his dream at any other time in the semester.

He plugged in his laptop and navigated to the slides for today—how the Constitution affected laws. Probably the last thing his students wanted to discuss.

Reaching behind him, he dimmed the lights in the room and stepped out from behind the lectern, gripping the microphone. He flicked it on and cleared his throat. "If you checked the syllabus, you know we're going to delve into the Constitution today and how it affects criminal justice. We'll start with the Sixth Amendment, but we'll cover the Fourth, Fifth, and Eighth before we're done."

He detected a few groans among the clicks and taps as the students readied their laptops and notebooks for class. A few students even took notes on their phones. Whatever worked.

Finn'd received high marks from students on the professor rating sites for keeping his classes lively and interesting, and he spent the next hour working extra hard to uphold his reputation. He'd managed to engage his students with the subject matter, but he always took questions at the end of the lecture. If he stopped now, they'd get suspicious.

He ended the slideshow and flooded the lecture hall with light. "Questions about the material we just covered?"

They managed to get through two questions about the Sixth Amendment, then the floodgates opened with the third question.

"Any news on Morgan's murder, Professor Karlsson?"

Everyone in the class started talking at once until he held up his hand. "I don't know any more than you all do, which means the police don't even have a person of interest yet. I want to remind you to be careful. Don't go out alone at night. Travel in packs and stay away from the forest."

He took a few more questions about the case that he couldn't answer, and then said, "One last question."

He paused for several seconds, waiting for the floor mic to make its way to the next and final student.

A woman cleared her throat. "Do you think Morgan Flemming's murder is connected to the murder of Tiffany Hunt ten years ago?"

A shot of adrenaline spiked through his system, and he jumped from the desk where he'd settled. "No! That's not possible. The Creekside Killer, Avery Plank, murdered Tiffany Hunt. He confessed."

The woman started to ask another question, but he cut her off. "That's it for today. Read chapters five through seven and email me a response to one of the amendments before class next week. It can be a set of questions or an analysis."

Finn's hand had a slight tremble as he turned his back

on the class and shoved some folders into his briefcase. He hadn't even discussed the Tiffany Hunt case in class yet. A lot of these students didn't even know about the murder, although most were familiar with the serial killer Avery Plank. Someone had been reading up on the university's crime stats.

"You didn't let me finish my question."

He spun around at the sound of the voice behind him, and he peered over the edge of the stage at the woman with one booted foot planted on the first step. From above, the wavy blond hair subdued into a ponytail lit a spark of recognition in his chest. When she tipped her head back and he met those luminous hazel eyes, he almost dropped his computer.

He took a deep breath, not wanting her to see that she'd rattled him. Lifting his shoulders, he slid his laptop into the bag on the desk. "We were running out of time, and there's not much more to discuss on the subject."

She climbed the remaining steps to the stage and squared off in front of him. "Oh, there's a lot more to discuss, Professor Karlsson… Deputy Karlsson, badge number 2852."

He narrowed his eyes as a muscle twitched at the corner of his mouth. "What are you doing back in school, Jessica? Looking to ruin more careers?"

"C'mon, this suits you so much better." She waved a hand at him. "You look good in civilian clothes, although you looked pretty good in that uniform, too."

His jaw tightened. "You don't need to resort to your fake flattery now. I have nothing to do with the Morgan Flemming case. I'm guessing you're here to stick your nose into the latest homicide on campus?"

"You make my interest in her murder sound so—" she rolled her eyes to the ceiling "—trivial."

"There's never anything trivial about any murder." He hoisted the satchel over his shoulder and ran a hand through his hair.

"I know that better than anyone." She caught her bottom lip between her teeth. "I found something at the crime scene."

About to brush past her, he tripped to a stop. "You were at the crime scene?"

"It's not off-limits anymore. Tape is down." She flicked her ponytail over her shoulder, and the golden waves danced and caught the light. "That's not the point. Did you hear what I said? I found something at the crime scene."

"Look, I know you're some hotshot forensic scientist now, but I'm pretty sure the deputies already went over that scene and didn't miss a thing."

Her eyes widened, and she tilted her head. "Really?"

He swallowed and jogged down the steps of the stage past her. Damn. How pathetic had he just made himself look by admitting he'd followed her career? He mumbled, "I've seen your name on a few local cases."

She snorted. "I meant really, are you so sure they didn't miss anything."

"If you found something at the scene, you'd better turn it over to the sheriff's department." He turned his back on her "You're a professional now, not a college student interfering in a case and causing trouble."

"Ah, Professor Karlsson?" One of his older students popped up from a seat in the front row. Had he heard the embarrassing exchange between him and Jessica?

"Mr. Webb, right?"

"Dermott Webb." The student's gaze traveled between him and Jessica, still on the stage. "Can I ask you a quick question about the assignment?"

"Of course." Finn tried to plaster a pleasant smile on his face.

"If we do some additional reading on the subject, can we use that material for our response instead of the textbook?" Webb held up his hand as if expecting him to deny the request. "I'd cite the reference material, of course."

"Yeah, yeah. That's fine if it sticks with the topic." Now he knew why he remembered this particular student. Finn always had one or two know-it-alls in a class, trying to impress or brownnose. Dermott Webb would probably make a good, by-the-book cop. The kind that would have the brass salivating.

"Thank you, Professor Karlsson. I'd like to talk with you further about this book—" his gaze darted toward Jessica again, now crossing her arms and tapping the toe of her boot "—I-I mean, during your office hours."

"Looking forward to hearing about it, Mr. Webb." Finn shifted slightly, showing Webb his shoulder in a broad hint.

"I'll see you in your office, then." Webb lifted his hand and loped from the lecture hall, excitement quickening his steps.

Raising her eyebrows, Jessica said, "Don't like him much, do you?"

"You can see my expression from the stage? The lights aren't even all the way up."

"No, I couldn't make out your face, but I know that tone of voice. You used it with me, once…"

"Once I found out you were manipulating me?" He rolled his shoulders. He shouldn't let her get under his skin. That way lay danger. "Don't you have some evidence to turn over to the sheriff's department?"

"Who said I'm not giving it to law enforcement? Hell, I *am* law enforcement." She bypassed the steps and jumped off the edge of the stage, landing in front of him, her hiking boots echoing in the empty hall. "But I'm willing to show it to you first…if you're interested."

He sucked in a quick breath. "Why the offer?"

"Because I have something to prove to you." She hooked a thumb in the belt loop of her slouchy jeans. "Buy you a drink?"

"It's the least you owe me, and I admit I'm curious." He patted the side of his bag. "Let me drop this at my office first, and I'll meet you at the Porch. I should be safe from my students there, even at this hour."

"Even the eager Mr. Webb?" She flicked her fingers in the air. "I know where the Porch is. I'll head over there now, Professor."

She made a beeline for the side door of the lecture hall, her blond ponytail swinging behind her, looking every bit the college student.

Finn exited through the back door, crossed the north campus quad and breathed a sigh of relief when he rounded the corner to an empty hallway. He didn't have office hours right now, but that didn't stop desperate students from dropping by to find out how they could turn in a late assignment or pick up some extra credit for a poor test score.

He unlocked his door and swung his bag onto the visitor chair opposite his desk. Then he locked up and strode across campus to exit on the north side, onto the bustling tree-lined street that boasted rows of bars and cheap eats, catering to the student crowd.

Finn veered off the street where it dead-ended at the path along the river and made his way to the more refined area of town that satisfied the palates and sensibilities of the parents who dropped their kids off—not expecting them to get murdered.

By the time he pushed through the front door of the Porch, Jessica had secured a table by the window. She wiggled her fingers in the air to draw his attention—as if he could ever miss Jessica Eller. As he approached the table, he pointed at the bar, and she shook her head.

He pulled out a chair and joined her. "Did you order already?"

"There's a waitress circulating. I told her to come back when my date got here."

He raised one eyebrow at her. "This isn't a date."

"Nobody has to know our business." She waved at the circulating waitress, and the woman, thank God not one of his students, ambled to their table.

The waitress tapped one elaborately painted nail on the Formica. "Did you see the happy hour menu?"

Finn picked up the plastic card and ran a finger down the list of beers. "I'll have the local IPA."

Jessica answered. "House white for me and some water, please."

Finn watched the waitress approach the bar and then planted his elbows on the table. "What did the cops and your CSI coworkers miss?"

Jessica plucked her cocktail napkin from the table and rummaged in the big bag on the seat beside her. Her hand emerged with a greeting card pinched between two fingers, covered by the napkin. She dropped it onto the table in front

of him. "I found this at Morgan's memorial site, where her
body was discovered."

He eyed the card, adorned with purple and yellow flowers, the word "condolences" in fancy gold script across the
front. He grabbed a knife and flicked open the card.

"Read it," Jessica demanded.

He cleared his throat and read aloud. "Something old,
something dead, something stolen, something red. So sorry
you had to join the club, Morgan. Love, Tiffany H."

Chapter Two

When the last word left Finn's lips, Jessica clapped both hands over her mouth, the shock of hearing her sister's name being connected to Morgan's murder hitting her square in the chest all over again. She hadn't imagined the words that had danced before her eyes out there in the woods.

Two lines formed between Finn's eyebrows as he pinned the open card to the table with the knife. "Were the other cards there as pristine as this one?"

She eked out a breath between her lips. He'd realized the card's importance instead of dismissing it. "No. The damp and dew had gotten to the other cards. When did the memorial form?"

"When the department removed the crime scene tape, about four days ago. This—" he nudged the card with the knife "—hasn't been there that long."

"Someone left it recently, maybe even this morning." Jessica hunched her shoulders against the shiver weaving up her spine. She could've just missed the guy out there.

She flinched when the waitress appeared with their drinks. Jessica pinched the stem of the glass between her fingers and raised it to her lips as Finn waved off the waitress's offer to pour his beer into a glass.

Closing her eyes, she sipped the wine, the crisp, bright flavor at odds with the subject between them. "What do you think?"

Finn took his time, studying the label on his bottle before taking a long drink. "It could be a tasteless joke."

"What about that rhyme? What does that all mean? Something stolen? Red?"

"No clue." He lifted his shoulders to his ears.

"D-do people around here still remember Tiffany's murder?" Jessica had come to the realization years ago that other people had moved on from her sister's homicide, even Ashley King and Denny Phelps, Tiffany's best friend and boyfriend at the time. She didn't have that luxury.

"Sure they do." Finn took another pull from his beer. "It's not like the campus has a murder every year, but they remember her as one of Avery Plank's victims."

"But join the club? Not Plank's club." She poked at the card with her fork. "Plank is in prison. He didn't kill Morgan, so what club is this?"

"The murder club. You're overthinking it, Jessica. Yeah, it's creepy, it's crude and rude, but it doesn't mean anything."

"You're not a cop anymore, Finn. You've lost the instinct." She swirled her wine in her glass.

"According to you, I never had that instinct."

Her gaze flew to his face as her cheeks turned pink. "I was just striking out. You were the one who found Tiffany's body, so I always connected you to the case. When the detectives wouldn't listen to me, I turned my wrath on you."

"Is that what you were doing?" He raised one eyebrow. "'Cuz I remember it differently. You hounded me, you played me, you stole from me, you compromised your own sister's case."

Burying her chin in her palm, she studied him as he took another sip of his beer. "I didn't compromise the case. Law enforcement had tunnel vision for Avery Plank."

"I don't know what to tell you." He spread his hands, a little calloused for an academic. "Plank confessed."

She flicked her fingers in the air. "Serial killers always exaggerate their numbers. You know that. What if Plank was lying? What if my sister's killer is still active…and he just hit again?"

"Ten years is a long time between kills," he said.

"Could be any number of reasons for that." She hunched forward, tucking a lock of hair behind her ear. "This could be a sick joke, but why bring Tiffany's name up at all?"

Finn rasped his knuckles across the scruff on his strong jaw, and Jessica glanced down at her wine. Ten years was also a long time between conversations with Finn Karlsson. Back when Tiffany was murdered, Jessica'd had a hard time separating her rage and grief from her insane attraction to the young cop who'd found her sister's body.

She hadn't figured out if she'd been so angry with him because he refused to believe her theories about her sister's case or because he refused to act on the electricity that sizzled between them.

Finn had gotten even more attractive over the years—that boyish uncertainty replaced with a manly confidence—but did the spark still exist?

She raised her eyes to his, and that blue intensity sparked by interest and passion and excitement still kindled, making her insides flutter. Yep. Still there.

"What are you thinking?" She clutched her wineglass,

holding her breath. She knew she'd been right to bring this card to Finn.

He blinked, those stubby dark lashes a striking contrast to his light eyes. "Who says I'm thinking anything at all?"

"You look like you're about to pounce on something."

Shrugging, he ran his thumbnail through the foil label on his bottle, dashing her hopes. "What brings you out to Fairwood? Are you really working Morgan's case, or are you here to thrash yourself some more over your sister's death?"

"I didn't…" Jessica scooped in a deep breath and puffed it out through puckered lips. "The case came to our crime lab in Marysville. Seattle is swamped, so we're processing the bulk of the evidence, especially as there's no firearm involved or prints—that we know of yet."

"You don't do prints in Marysville?"

He cocked his head, that light in his eyes signaling his attention and sincerity. Maybe that's why she'd homed in on him ten years ago as the go-to guy for her wild theories. He'd actually listened to her ranting. Of course, that's what had gotten him in trouble.

"No prints in Marysville. DNA and materials analysis only." She thumped her chest with her palm. "That's me."

"You do materials analysis for the forensics lab?" He nodded. "That makes total sense. You could find a chip of paint on a rock of the same color."

"Or—" she used her napkin to slide the condolence card into an envelope "—a creepy card at a memorial site."

"How much material evidence was collected at the scene of Morgan's murder?"

She put a finger to her lips. "I'm not supposed to reveal that information. I haven't even gotten a look at it yet, anyway. It's already been collected at the sheriff's station."

"You'll get a list of it, though, right? Maybe I should steal it from you?" Finn sat back and crossed his arms. "Turnabout is fair play."

She dragged her gaze away from his broad shoulders. Had he gotten that buff carrying around books?

"Look, my little speech before? That was meant to be an apology." She held up her hands. "I know it's a little late and I know I ruined your career, but I was running on pure emotion and…"

He rapped on the table, and she snapped her mouth shut. "You did not ruin my career. Straight police work was never a good fit for me. I've always had a problem following orders, sort of like you."

"You think I'm going rogue investigating outside the parameters of my job?" She lifted her shoulders. "Not my fault the original crime scene investigators missed some material evidence."

"Even you agree that card was most likely left at the scene after the fact. They didn't miss it."

"Which actually proves my point—I'm not out of bounds here. Anyone could've found that card. It just happened to be me." She tilted her glass to her lips, eyeing Finn over the rim as he folded his hands around his bottle, the label in shreds. "What's wrong?"

"I'm just thinking what a coincidence it is—you're the one who finds the card with the reference to your sister."

"And?" She twirled her finger in the air. "What are you driving at?"

"Haven't you gotten to the point in your law enforcement career where you've learned nothing is a coincidence?"

Jessica's jaw dropped. "Do you think I planted this to… to…get attention? Reopen my sister's case?"

"Whoa, slow down with the assumptions." He formed a cross with his two index fingers. "Did anyone know you were coming out here to have a look around the crime scene?"

She swallowed. Took a sip of wine and swallowed again. "My coworkers know I'm here."

"Would it be hard for an outsider to figure it out? Do you post on social media, stuff like that?"

"I rarely use social media and definitely wouldn't broadcast my work schedule or location for everyone to see." She pinged her fingernail against her almost-empty wineglass. "You're suggesting that someone left it for me, specifically."

Tapping the side of his head, he said, "Don't tell me that steel-trap mind of yours didn't suspect that when you found it."

A breath whispered across the back of her neck, and Jessica pressed a hand against her heart pounding in her chest. She *had* thought that.

"So, it crossed your mind."

She gulped down the last sip of wine. "It did. Why would Morgan's killer want to tease me like this if he weren't also connected to Tiffany's death?"

"Hang on." Finn splayed his hands on the table, thumbs touching. "We don't know that it was Morgan's killer who left the card, and even if it was her killer who left it, that still doesn't mean he had anything to do with Tiffany's murder. He could be playing games with you, with the cops."

"Creepy either way." She dragged her purse into her lap and shoved her hand inside to grab her wallet. "I'm going back there."

"Wait. What?" Finn's blue eyes widened. "Now?"

"Maybe he knows I took the card. Maybe he's still hanging around there. Maybe he left another clue."

"You think you're going to catch him in the act?" He tossed a few bills on the table before she could open her wallet. "I know I mentioned coincidence, but that's not gonna happen."

Leveling a finger at him, she asked, "Don't you want to see where I found it?"

"You're inviting me to come along?"

"Would be good to get a cop's…an ex-cop's perspective on that altar to Morgan."

"You just told me I'd lost my cop's instincts."

"That sort of thing never goes away, does it? You had it back then, that's how you found Tiffany, and you still have it." She dropped her wallet back into her purse. "Let's go."

They headed for Finn's vehicle, which enjoyed a parking place on campus. As they approached the mud-splashed Jeep, Jessica said, "I see you still enjoy the outdoors."

"Took a trip this past weekend. Didn't have time to clean it up before class." He opened the passenger door for her. "Don't mind the dog hair. Bodhi rides shotgun."

He slammed the door, and she brushed a little light-colored fur from the seat. If his dog rode shotgun, that probably meant he didn't have a wife—not that she hadn't already surreptitiously checked out his left hand.

He slid behind the wheel and started the engine. "I'm not sure what you expect to find out there."

"Can't tell you, but after I found the card, I got out of there. I felt like I was being watched, didn't give myself a chance to look at the other items." She clasped her hands between her knees. "Maybe I meant to take you back there with me all along."

"Yeah, barging into my lecture hall shooting questions at me is the way to do it."

"Bought you a beer, didn't I?"

"I paid for those drinks."

"Oh, yeah. Next round's on me."

He gave her a glance from the side of his eye, but his lip quirked upward. Maybe he liked that idea.

They stopped talking, each immersed in their own thoughts, as Finn drove the short distance to the crime scene—Morgan's crime scene. Earlier, Jessica had parked near her sister's murder site and followed the river on foot to Morgan's. This time, they traversed the trail to Morgan's memorial in about ten minutes.

The same eerie feeling permeated the air, even with Finn tromping on the trail behind her. The forest seemed to be holding its breath, the critters silent and watchful.

The sound of the gurgling river broke the stillness, and Jessica quickened her pace. Daylight still filtered through the tops of the trees, but the long shadows signaled the setting of the sun. She didn't want to be there in the dark— Finn or no Finn.

She almost tripped into the clearing, and Finn put a hand on her hip. "You okay?"

"Maybe we should've waited until morning for this expedition." She rubbed the goose bumps on her arms, pretty sure they'd popped up because of the location and not Finn's touch.

"Let's make this quick." He flung an arm out toward the pile of teddy bears and flowers. "You have a look at the cards again, and I'll take some pictures with my phone that you can study later."

"The stuff looks like it's been moved around since this afternoon." Jessica ran her tongue around her dry mouth.

"How can you tell?" Finn marched toward the memorial, pulling his phone from his pocket.

She followed him, dragging her feet. As she crouched next to the mound of memorial items left with the best of intentions, she reached for the cards she'd stacked earlier.

She glimpsed a black button eye from the depths of the pile, and her hands froze. With trembling fingers, she nudged aside the stuffed animals and candles to reveal the doll, staring at her from the center of the heap with its single eye.

Falling back in the dirt, she let out a piercing cry.

"What's wrong?" Finn swung around.

"That doll." She pointed a finger at the dirty rag doll with yellow braids and a red-checked blouse.

"Kind of odd, but what's the problem? Maybe Morgan had a thing for rag dolls." He cocked his head and dropped to his knees beside her. "You're really spooked."

She dragged her gaze away from the horrifying sight and clutched Finn's arm. "You don't understand. That's *my* doll. My childhood doll."

Chapter Three

"Wait." Finn jabbed his finger in the direction of the rag doll. "You're saying that's a doll you had when you were a kid? Like, that was the actual doll you owned?"

Jessica's grip on his arm tightened, and her fingernails dug into his skin through his shirt. "I-I don't know. I don't understand."

"Maybe it just looks like the same doll." Using a stick, Finn nudged the other items out of the way and slid the doll's clothing to lift it from the pile. As it swung in the air, pigtails flying, Jessica pressed a hand over her mouth.

He dropped the doll at their feet, and Jessica shifted away from it as if it would bite her with its smiling red mouth. "Is it the same *type* of doll you had as a child?"

His mind refused to entertain the thought that this was Jessica's doll. This place had her all rattled—not that he could blame her.

She sniffed. "It's not the same doll. Mine was dirty. This one is brand-new, but look."

He peered over her shoulder as she pointed a shaky finger at the missing button on the doll's face.

He said, "Yeah, not brand-new."

"It's the button, Finn. My doll was missing the same button eye. Somebody placed this doll, a replica of the only doll I had as a child, on Morgan's memorial. Why? How?"

Squeezing his eyes closed and pinching the bridge of his nose, Finn asked, "Who would even know about this doll?"

"Tiffany...and maybe a few of her friends." Jessica clasped a hand around the long column of her throat, one tear sparkling on the ends of her lashes. "When I went away to college in Oregon and Tiffany got the job here, I gave her my doll. I didn't want to leave her once she got her life on track, but she insisted I take the scholarship. So maybe it is the same doll...the doll I gave to Tiffany."

"Okay, okay. That makes some sense." Finn released a noisy breath. "Maybe Morgan's murder, because of the location so close to Tiffany's, triggered one of Tiffany's friends and she put the doll here, thinking it was Tiffany's doll. Maybe this same person left the card."

Jessica pulled her plump lower lip between her teeth. "I suppose that could've happened. But..."

"But what?" Finn held his breath, preparing himself for Jessica's next outlandish proposal.

"What if Tiffany's killer took the doll at the time of her murder and planted it here?" Using the stick, Jessica picked up the doll.

"There was never any evidence that Tiffany's killer had been inside her place—no fingerprints there, no DNA, no signs of a struggle or break-in. He ambushed her by the side of the creek and used a garrote to strangle her, one we never found."

"Morgan was strangled, too."

"Just like every other victim of the Creekside Killer. Maybe what we have with Morgan is a copycat." He prodded the doll with his fingertip. "Are you taking this with you? You know, even though you're bagging this stuff, you've ruined the chain of custody. An attorney would destroy this evidence in court."

"Thanks for telling me my job. I'm still taking it in, along with that card. This is personal." She scooped up the doll by its midsection, squeezing the soft material with her hand. "I'm going to look up Ashley and Denny, Tiffany's friends, and find out what they know about this doll."

"Did you look for it when—" Finn coughed "—when you came to collect Tiffany's property?"

"I'd forgotten about it. Tiffany didn't have many possessions, nothing of monetary value. I kept a few pieces of her cheap costume jewelry, just for sentimental reasons, but I'd forgotten I gave her the doll. This is all so creepy." Jessica pushed to her feet, brushing the dirt from her jeans, and tilted her head back to examine the trees that ringed the site. "I wonder if it would be worth it at this point to set up cameras here."

"Not a bad idea. I know law enforcement attends funerals and memorial services for the same reason—to see if the killer makes an appearance." Finn planted his feet more firmly on the dirt, as he felt his world tilt just a little. Jessica Eller was drawing him into her vortex of the fantastic once again. "I'm not saying Morgan's killer left these items, but video of someone leaving them would be useful. Someone's definitely playing some games here."

"Or worse." She tucked the doll under her arm, its floppy legs dangling over her hip. "I might just meet with the sheriff's department and ask them about the possibility of setting up a camera out here. I need to talk to the CSI first on the scene, anyway."

Holding up his phone, he asked, "Are you ready to go? I took quite a few pictures. I'll send them to you. Number?"

His thumb hovered over the number pad on his phone through the silence. Did she think this was a ruse to get her cell phone number? He glanced up, but she wasn't paying any attention to him.

She'd turned on her toes, looking like a deer ready to flee, peering into the forest.

His pulse thrummed. "Do you see something?"

She whipped around, clutching the doll to her chest. "Probably just the night critters stirring. We should get out of here before we have to scuff back through the trees with just our puny cell phone flashlights to guide us."

He pocketed his phone. He'd get her number later. If he didn't get her away from this place before the sun went down, he'd probably have to carry her back to the car.

Jessica led the way back to the road, her long legs eating up the trail. Finn almost had to jog to keep up with her. By the time they reached the road where he'd parked his car, he had to stop to catch his breath.

Wiping the back of his hand across his brow, he said, "You really wanted out of there."

"The whole place makes my skin crawl." She threw a fearful glance over her shoulder at the tree line. "Even more than ever."

She still clutched the doll in her hand, and he nodded at it. "That thing is going to be useless as evidence."

"You're probably right." She held the doll in front of her and met its button eye, as if she could read some clue buried in the inanimate object. "But I'm going to get to the bottom of why someone left these items at the memorial, one way or another."

Their feet crunched the gravel on the shoulder of the road as they walked back to his car…at a normal pace. He got the door for her, noticing a slight trembling of her hand.

Pointing into the back seat, he said, "There are a couple of bottles of water back there. You look like you could use one."

He slammed the door and circled to the driver's side. He slid behind the wheel, and she tapped his arm with the neck of the plastic bottle. "Can you open this for me? My hands are a little sweaty."

"Must be that race you ran through the woods back there. I could hardly keep up." He took the bottle from her and cracked the seal on the cap. "Do you want to give me your cell phone number? I'll send you the pictures I took."

"Sure." She put the bottle to her lips and gulped down some water while he fumbled for his cell.

"Ready." When she finished, she rattled off her phone number.

"I'll send them when I get home." He started the engine and rested his hands on the steering wheel. "Back to your car?"

"Yeah, it's parked on the east side of campus."

"Are you staying in town or headed back to… Marysville? Is that where you live?"

"I actually live in Seattle but do a lot of my work in Marysville. The lab in Seattle gets bogged down with tons of cases, and it handles firearms on top of everything else. Due to the workload there, we often take care of materials in Marysville."

He whistled through his teeth. "You're going to hit some traffic, and depending on the ferry schedule it could take you a few hours to get home."

"That's why I'm staying here in town. I have a hotel room down by the water." She shrugged. "My boss wants me to meet with the sheriffs while I'm here. I have a massive to-do list right now."

Finn wheeled out onto the road. "What's first on your list? Meeting with the deputies?"

"That can wait. The material evidence isn't going anywhere." She clasped her hands between her knees and turned to stare out the window. "There's something else I need to do first. Someone I need to see."

"Tiffany's friends? Have you looked them up yet?"

"Ashley and Denny can wait, too." She grabbed the bottle of water and twisted the cap. "But Avery Plank can't."

Finn jerked his head to the side, and the car swerved into the gravel for a few seconds. "You're going to visit Avery Plank in the pen?"

"I've already cleared it. He's expecting me tomorrow during visiting hours." She sloshed the water around in the bottle, its motion mirroring his thoughts.

"Why on earth would you want to talk to Plank?" Finn smacked his palms on the steering wheel. "Wait. Have you seen him before?"

"Never. This is my first visit, although I've been thinking about it for a while. I even wrote a few letters to him that I ripped up."

"He's dangerous, Jessica." He jerked his thumb over his shoulder. "You felt evil at Morgan's death site. Wait until you sit across from Plank. You'll choke on it."

She tipped some water into her mouth and licked her lips. "He's locked up. He can't hurt me."

"Here." Finn tapped the side of his head. "He'll hurt you

up here. He plays games with people. You're not going to get any truth out of him."

"You sure didn't feel that way about him ten years ago, did you? None of you did." She put on a fake low voice as she said, "Oh, hey, Avery, did you kill Tiffany Hunt? Shari Chang? Letitia Rocha? You wanna help us close some pesky open cases we couldn't be bothered to investigate?"

"Those cases didn't come out of the blue. They all had the same pattern as the Creekside Killer victims. It made sense." He clenched his jaw. It *had* been the easy way out, but it didn't mean law enforcement was wrong or that Plank was lying.

"Okay, so you all believed him then. But *now* I'm not going to get any truth out of him?" She pushed her wheat-colored hair out of her face. "What if Plank tells me the same thing he told law enforcement all those years ago? What if he tells me he did murder my sister? Is he to be trusted again because he gave the acceptable answer?"

Finn opened his mouth a few times like a fish out of water. She wasn't wrong, but he had his own reasons for keeping her away from Plank. "He'll toy with you, and he'll enjoy it. Will he know who you are tomorrow? Did you indicate you were a victim's sister on your request or just that you worked for the Washington State Patrol?"

"Both." She narrowed her hazel eyes. "I wanted to make sure I got in."

"The family of one of his victims?" Finn shook his head. "He'll go to town on you. When you walk out of there, you're not gonna know which way is up."

Jessica folded her hands in her lap, her knuckles white. "You underestimate me, Finn. You know what my childhood was like. Do you really think a man like Avery Plank is going to rattle me? Hell, a guy like that could've been one of my stepfathers."

He swallowed. She'd told him all about growing up with a drug-addicted mother and the men who populated their lives…and the older half sister who'd protected her from all of it. At the time, he thought she'd given him a sob story to sway him, get him to do things for her that a young patrol officer should've never done.

When she disappeared from his life and he got over his anger, he did some investigating and discovered every word she'd told him had been the truth. It made him ache for her all over again.

"I know you had it bad when you were a kid. Know your mom exposed you to all kinds of unsavory people, but Plank is evil."

"Gee, a serial killer is evil. Thanks, Sherlock. I'm not going to be sitting down for tea and scones with him. He'll be chained up like the animal he is." She rapped one knuckle on the window. "Turn right on this street. I'm up one block."

Finn took the turn onto a tree-lined street that bordered the eastern edge of the campus. Night had fallen, and the towering Douglas firs blocked out most of the streetlights, creating a shadowy tunnel where few cars remained.

The university had a call-in system where students could request an escort to their cars, but few vehicles parked on this street at this time of night. The library sat on the other side of campus, around the corner from a hub of restaurants, bars and shops.

After Morgan's murder, the Safe Line had been getting a massive number of calls. Tonight, he'd be Jessica's safe line.

"That's me." Jessica pointed to a green Subaru parked

on the left side of the street, so Finn made a U-turn at the next intersection and pulled behind her car.

He cut the engine and opened his door as Jessica unclasped her seat belt.

"You don't have to get out, but I'd appreciate it if you watched while I get into my car and start it."

"It's not a problem. I'll just take a quick look around your car before you get in. Nice ride." He pushed out of the car while she grabbed her stuff.

She beeped her remote, and the lights flashed and stayed on while he peered into the back seat. He skirted the trunk and stepped onto the sidewalk, surveying the side of her vehicle, which seemed to tilt in the back.

He swore under his breath. He didn't even need to crouch down to see the problem. "Ah, Jessica. You're gonna want to have a look at this before you start that engine."

Leaving the driver's-side door open, she joined him on the sidewalk. "What now?"

He leveled a finger at her back tire. "You've got a flat."

She hunched forward, reaching out her hand toward the wheel. She ran her fingers over the rubber and cranked her head over her shoulder, the whites of her rounded eyes gleaming in the dark. "It's flat because someone slashed it."

Chapter Four

Her fingertips traced the smooth edge of the cut in her tire. What would've happened if Finn hadn't noticed the tire and she drove back to her hotel on it? Would she have made it? Would she have been compelled to stop the car to check on it?

"Someone not only knows I'm here, but this person also knows my car or maybe has been following me." She sat back on her heels, inspecting her smudged fingers. "You know I'm right. What did you say earlier about coincidences?"

He crouched beside her, bumping her shoulder. "Somebody is trying to scare you."

"Scare? The card and the doll were meant to scare or maybe even send a message, but this? She rubbed her fingertips on the wet grass beside the curb. "A slashed tire could've caused me to stop the car on the way back to the hotel, or maybe even have caused an accident. I think we've moved beyond psychological terror now."

Finn rose to his feet and stepped into the road, tilting his head back. "Too far from campus to have any cameras on this street, but maybe one of the apartment complexes farther up the block has something pointed this way. I can check for you tomorrow. It might be as simple as identifying this guy and making him stop."

"Or not." Jessica lifted her hatchback and peeled back the flooring. "I have a spare, if you want to help me."

"Or we can leave your car here and take care of it tomorrow in the light of day. I can give you a ride back to your hotel tonight, and then back again to your car."

"I appreciate the offer, but you forget. I have a meeting with a serial killer tomorrow, and I need to leave here by five in the morning to get to the pen in plenty of time for my one o'clock appointment."

"You're making the five-hour drive to Walla Walla?" Finn clasped the back of his neck. "Why not take an hour flight from Seattle?"

"I drive all over the state." She shrugged, not wanting to admit to Finn that she avoided flying when she could. She was supposed to be presenting a front of fearlessness.

"That's crazy. I'll book you on a flight tomorrow, and I'll come with you."

"Why would you do that?" Could it be that Finn was starting to believe Avery Plank didn't commit Tiffany's homicide, or did he want to horn in on her interview of Plank to guide the outcome?

"Because I don't think you should do this on your own, and I'm sure as hell not sitting in a car for five hours."

Crossing her arms, she planted her boots on the asphalt. "And I'm sure as hell not allowing you to sit in on my interview with Plank. I'm talking to him by myself."

"I don't want to be there while you talk to Plank, but I do want to be there when you get out of that hellhole. You shouldn't be on your own, and you really shouldn't spend five hours driving by yourself musing on Avery Plank. We can get you a new tire early tomorrow morning and head to the airport right after."

She screwed up the side of her mouth, studied Finn's handsome face and relented. "Have it your way. When did you get so bossy?"

"About ten years ago after I got bamboozled by some doe-eyed teenager."

"I was twenty-one."

"That doesn't make it better." He nodded at her disabled vehicle. "Do you have all your stuff?"

She jogged to her car and ducked inside, grabbing her purse and that cursed doll from the passenger seat. As she locked up, she said, "I hope my stalker doesn't return to do more damage."

"Stalker? I hope not."

"I hope that's all he is."

Back in his car, she directed Finn to her hotel by the water, and he insisted on walking her inside the lobby. She wasn't about to refuse this time.

She waved at the hotel clerk and pointed to the elevator. "I think I got this."

"I'll look into a morning flight, and we'll take care of your car before we head out." He touched her arm. "Thanks for coming to me with the card. I'll do what I can."

"Well, you've already gone above and beyond. Thank *you*. I didn't expect it."

"Get a good night's sleep. I'll call you around seven."

Finn planted himself in the lobby as Jessica walked to the elevator. She turned when the doors opened and lifted her hand before stepping inside.

She hadn't expected Finn to be so interested in her theories about Morgan's case and its connection to Tiffany's.

He'd explained it as concern for her, but something about his concern rang false.

Finn Karlsson was no longer the sweet, gullible man she'd met ten years ago. His baby-blue eyes held secrets, and she was determined to discover them...even if it meant putting her heart in danger again.

THE FOLLOWING MORNING had been such a whirlwind of changing her tire, driving to the shop to get a new one to replace her spare and rushing to the airport to catch their last-minute flight to Walla Walla, Jessica's anxiety about flying hadn't had a minute to manifest itself. Now, as the jet's engines roared beneath her and the plane lifted, she dug her fingernails into the armrest.

She could use one of those canned Bloody Marys from the drink cart, but she didn't want Finn to think she was a morning drinker. She also didn't want to have alcohol on her breath when she went to the prison. She squeezed her eyes closed.

Finn bumped her shoulder. "Are you all right? I'm sure I can work something out with the prison and go inside with you."

Ugh. He assumed her nerves were all about meeting Plank. She loosened her death grip on the armrest and flexed her fingers. "Not a fan of taking off."

"I'm okay with taking off. I don't like landing." He bent forward and dragged his laptop case from beneath the seat in front of him. "Do you mind if I do some work? I canceled a class today, but I still have some papers to grade."

She hated landing only slightly less than taking off. "Go ahead. Really, you didn't have to do all of this. I could've changed the tire last night and driven down on my spare this morning."

He widened his eyes. "You're not meant to drive three hundred miles on a spare."

"Just do your grading." She flicked her fingers at his laptop, now open on his tray table. "I have some notes to review."

She reached up and pressed the light button with her knuckle and pulled her purse into her lap. Digging around in the depths of her bag, she found her notebook and flipped it open. She scanned the words she'd scrawled on the page weeks ago, more to give herself something to do than as a review. She didn't even need this notebook. She'd had these questions memorized for almost ten years.

The airplane dipped and she gasped, closing her eyes and clutching the notebook to her chest. After a few seconds of smooth sailing, she opened one eye, feeling Finn's attention from the seat next to hers.

He whispered, "Probably just a pocket of air." He closed his laptop. "Did I ever tell you the story about the Ferris wheel at the state fair?"

"No." She threaded her fingers together and pressed her hands against her midsection.

"I had been on all the hair-raising rides all afternoon, even while I filled up on cotton candy and chili dogs and kettle corn and funnel cake. But when night fell, I heard a girl from school wanted to go on the Ferris wheel with me." He rubbed his hands together. "As a randy fifteen-year-old boy, I figured I'd just gotten lucky."

She turned her head. "And did you? Get lucky, I mean."

"Absolutely not."

Finn then proceeded to tell her a story about his abject

fear of riding the Ferris wheel and trying to impress this girl. Even though Jessica was sure he'd embellished the tale, he had her giggling and covering her eyes at his humiliation.

He followed that story with another about the first time he went scuba diving, which had tears rolling down her face. He'd obviously conquered all these fears because she knew from before that he was an adventurous outdoorsman.

While she mopped her face with the napkin from the Diet Coke she'd ordered, she heard a loud clunk and clapped her hand to her chest. "What was that?"

"The landing gear. We're getting ready to touch down." He gave an exaggerated grimace. "I told you this is my least favorite part of flying."

"Do you want me to hold your hand?" She patted his hand, resting on his laptop. "We don't want a repeat of the Ferris wheel debacle. You did eat a lot of pretzels."

He held out his hand, palm up. "Please."

She slid her palm on top of his palm, curling her fingers around his hand. "Just this once. You're gonna have to learn to suck it up."

Even though she knew he was pretending fear to make her feel better, it worked. Or maybe it was the feel of his warm, rough skin against hers. She swooned, along with the plane, but she welcomed the butterflies as long Finn held her hand.

"Thanks." He grinned as he shoved his computer back into its case with his other hand and nudged it beneath the seat with his foot.

As the airplane whooshed downward, Finn squeezed her hand, and she didn't mind at all—not even when the wheels touched down.

When the plane came to a stop, they unclipped their seat belts and gathered their bags. She poked Finn in the back as they made their way off the plane. "Thanks."

"Yeah, I can't believe a woman who isn't afraid to face Avery Plank is afraid to fly."

She shrugged as she hitched her bag over her shoulder. "I can't control what happens up here."

"If you think you can control Avery Plank, you're in for a big surprise." He clicked his tongue. "It's only a ten-minute drive to the pen. Let's grab some lunch in town before heading out there."

They collected the rental car at the airport and Jessica checked her phone for a restaurant on the way to the pen. Ten minutes later, they were seated at a sandwich shop in the middle of town with a couple of paper cups filled with soda.

Finn sat back and folded his arms. "Are you going to flat out ask Plank if he killed your sister?"

"That's the point." She plunged her straw into her second Diet Coke of the day, already feeling wired.

"Do you expect to hear the truth from him, and how will you know it when you hear it?"

"I'll worry about all that when I get to it. I have to do this. I have to look in his eyes."

"You're not gonna like what you see there. Plank—" he coughed "—all these guys—have dead eyes."

"You don't have to tell me that." She cocked her head. "They just called our number. You get the sandwiches, and I'll fill up our drinks."

She scooted from the booth before Finn could come up with more reasons why she shouldn't meet with Plank. Why did he care so much? She could maintain her composure around Plank. In her career with Washington's Crime Laboratory Division, she'd been to plenty of crime scenes, had seen more blood than she cared to remember and had testified at the trials of gruesome killers. She could handle sitting across from a chained-up murderer past his prime— even if he had confessed to killing her sister.

For the remainder of the lunch, Jessica peppered Finn with questions about his classes, mostly to keep him away from the subject of Avery Plank, but he'd held her interest with his account of the lessons he gave his students and how he engaged them.

When she'd first met Finn ten years ago, the deputy who'd discovered her sister's body, she'd often wondered what it would be like between them without the secrets, lies and deception on her part. Now she knew that it could be something special.

Back then, she'd manipulated him into giving her information about the scene and evidence that he was in no position to reveal. She'd used him, even as she was falling hard for him. That same care he'd had for her ten years ago had never gone away.

"Ready?" She bunched up the waxy paper from her sandwich and dropped it on the red plastic tray on the side of the table. "I want to make sure I'm on time."

"If I can't talk you out of it, I guess it's go time." He slid the tray from the table, dumped the trash and left the tray on top of the receptacle.

Once in the rental car, her hands trembled a little as she snapped her seat belt in place, but she told herself it was because of excitement, not fear.

They drove in silence for the brief ten-minute journey with wheat fields on either side of the road, and both handed over their ID at the guard shack in the front beneath the arched sign that heralded penitentiary grounds. The green grass looked inviting, but the facade ended at the gray-and-brown stone building with the watchtower surveying the area.

Finn parked the car and stayed seated. "I'm going to wait here…unless you want me to go inside with you."

She licked her dry lips. "No. I'm good. See you in about an hour."

Once inside the prison admin building, Jessica went through the paperwork, the body scan and the pat-down. The low heels of her black boots tapped on the linoleum floor on the way to the visitor center as she followed the buff form of the corrections officer.

He opened the door and guided her to a table in the middle of the room. Empty chairs and love seats littered the space, and two baskets filled with toys stood sentry on either side of a colorful carpet.

Twisting her fingers in front of her, Jessica asked, "No other visitors today?"

"Their appointment times are later. Usually when one of our high-profile inmates has a visitor, we clear out the room. Gary Ridgeway. Kenneth Bianchi." The CO shrugged his broad shoulders. "Just to be on the safe side. There will be one of us at each of the doors."

She gave him a jerky nod, and he pulled out one of the chairs stationed at the desk for her. She sat down and rubbed her palms against the thighs of her black slacks. The pen imposed a modest dress code, but she'd taken it a step further with her low-heeled shoes, professional pants, a blouse buttoned almost to the top of her neck and a loose-fitting jacket.

When the door opposite opened, she jumped in her seat. A CO led Plank into the room, his feet shuffling to accommodate the chains wrapping his ankles and attached to the cuffs around his wrists. They weren't taking any chances with this guy.

She eked out a small breath and folded her hands on the table in front of her, like a schoolteacher waiting for a recalcitrant pupil. She kept her gaze trained on Plank as he scuffed across the floor. She couldn't get over how average he looked. She wouldn't give the guy a second glance in the coffeehouse or the gym or the grocery store. That's how he'd taken his victims by surprise. Just an average dude doing average things—until he wasn't.

Just as she watched his approach, he kept his gaze trained on her…soaking her in. His attention was anything but average. His brown eyes darted across every inch of her visible body, measuring, weighing, judging—a predatory assessment that had her squeezing her folded hands tighter.

The CO who'd ushered her into the room kicked out the chair across from her. "You know the drill, Plank. Sit."

The Creekside Killer plopped into the chair facing her, his chains clanging and clinking. His guard ran a chain from the stationary table through his ankle and wrist bracelets, securing him in place—right in front of her.

Her hand shook as she dipped it into her pocket to fetch her phone. She'd been warned against taking photos, but she was allowed to record him with his assent.

Setting the phone on the table between them, she cleared her throat. "Hello, Mr. Plank. I'm Jessica Eller from the Washington State Patrol, Crime Lab Division. Do you mind if I record our conversation?"

Shaking his head from side to side, he blinked once,

a slow lowering of the lids over perceptive eyes. "You're that girl's sister, too." He snapped his fingers and rolled his eyes to the ceiling.

Jessica said her sister's name through her teeth. "Tiffany Hunt."

He leveled a long index finger at her, and she noticed for the first time that his hands were anything but average. They were huge, and Jessica flashed on an image of them wrapped around some poor woman's neck, squeezing the life out of her.

"That's right. Tiffany. She was a brunette, though, and you're a blonde." He cocked his head as if reviewing a lesson in genetics. "You sure you two were sisters? From what I read, your mother was a woman of low morals just like sweet Tiffany."

Jessica's cheek burned as if he'd slapped her. He knew about her mother, about her family. Would he bother with that if he hadn't killed Tiffany?

Raising his cuffed hands, he said, "Don't feel bad, Jessica. My mother was a whore, too."

She'd studied his psychological profile and knew all about his background, but why did he know about hers? She was ready for his attack this time, the ugly word, and didn't even blink an eye.

She tapped the record icon on her phone and straightened it on the table. "So, you did kill my sister."

"Did you have any doubt? I confessed to it."

"The MO was different from the others. Despite my sister's troubled past, she wasn't a sex worker at the time of her murder." She tightened her jaw. "And you didn't rape her, didn't leave your DNA."

"Ah, the outraged sister is also a crime investigator." He

folded his hands, mimicking her stance from before. "What else was different?"

"You didn't use your hands to strangle Tiffany." Her gaze bounced to his large mitts folded primly and back to his face, alert and bright. He was enjoying himself. "You didn't pose her. You didn't leave her nude."

He clapped his hands together, the cuffs on his wrists resulting in an incongruously dainty motion. "I'm impressed. You're very good, Jessica."

"I'm not here for your admiration, Plank. I don't think you killed my sister, but I can't figure out why you know so much about her life." She held her breath as Plank glanced over his shoulder at the CO.

Hunching across the table, he lowered his voice. "I make it my business to know the details of other cases in the same area as my...hunting ground."

She'd dipped her head to catch his words, and then jerked back as he finished his sentence, drawing the attention of the corrections officer by the door leading back to the cells. She met the CO's eyes and gave him a brief shake of her head.

She returned her focus to Plank and asked, "Does that mean you didn't kill Tiffany?"

He leaned back in his chair. "What about this girl Morgan?"

A chill rippled down the length of Jessica's spine. "You know about that murder?"

"What did I just tell you, Jessica?" He clicked his tongue. "It's my hobby."

"Do you think it's a Creekside Killer copycat?"

"Let's see." He held up one manacled hand, the cuff slipping from his wrist to his elbow. "No rape, strangled, but most likely with an object, and Morgan was a sweet little coed, not a lady of the night. If he's copying me, he's doing a poor job of it."

"So, you didn't murder Tiffany. Is that what you're saying?"

"You're getting dull, Jessica." He snapped his fingers. "I'll tell you what, you can read my book. Perhaps I'll reveal all amongst its pages."

She snorted. "You're not allowed to write a book about your crime and profit from it."

He gave a high-pitched giggle that made her skin crawl. "I'm an engineer, not a writer. Someone else is writing my story."

"I suppose there are all kinds of lowlifes willing to exploit murder for profit."

"Oh, come on, Jessica. Don't try to tell me you haven't read books about serial killers. There are a couple of them here at the pen who have been best-seller subjects. In fact—" he drummed his fingers on the table next to her phone "—you probably know this author."

"Doubt it." She glanced over Plank's shoulder at the CO twirling his finger in the air. Her time was almost up, and Plank hadn't given her a straight answer about Tiffany.

"Oh, no. I'm sure you know him or know *of* him. He's the cop who found your sister's body, although he's not on the job anymore."

Her attention snapped back to Plank. "Who? What are you saying?"

"I'm saying Professor Finn Karlsson is writing a book about me."

Chapter Five

Finn glanced at the clock in the lower-right corner of his computer screen. Jessica should be coming out soon. He doubted she got any satisfaction from Plank. The guy played games—and Finn knew that better than anyone at this point.

He squeezed the back of his neck and took a sip of the soda he'd refilled on his way out of the sandwich shop, now watery and lukewarm. From the corner of his eye, he caught sight of a figure moving toward him.

He slid his laptop into its case and jumped from the car to get Jessica's door. He squinted at her through his sunglasses. From the way she was practically marching across the parking lot, Plank had angered more than scared her. She probably didn't get a straight answer from him about Tiffany.

He wasn't about to go through the told-you-so routine with her.

As he opened the passenger door for her, she gave him a tight-lipped glance. Finn knew when to keep his mouth shut. He closed her door almost gently and took his time getting back to the driver's side.

Once behind the wheel, he gave her a sideways glance. "Didn't go well?"

She whipped her head around so fast her ponytail almost slapped her face. "Avery Plank is a liar and a game player."

"Yeah, he is."

Her hazel eyes turned to pools of dark green. "And you should know because so are you."

Finn scratched his chin. She knew. Either the COs or Plank himself told her. "Look, I didn't want to tell you about the book because I didn't want to upset you."

"How thoughtful." She grabbed the drink in the cup holder and shoved the straw in her mouth. Wrinkling her nose, she removed the lid and tossed the liquid out the window.

"That was my old soda. Do you want another?"

She crushed the paper cup in her hand. "I want you to tell me why you're writing this book. Y-you're exploiting the deaths of all those women, including Tiffany."

"Do you feel that way about other true crime books or just this one? There are probably a dozen books about the Hillside Strangler, a dozen about the Green River Killer—" he jerked his thumb over his shoulder at the prison where those two killers currently resided "—and I'm betting you read a few of each. Hell, you probably even watched the movies."

She dropped her chin to her chest, and her eyelashes fluttered. "He knew about Morgan Flemming."

"Of course he did. What did he say about Tiffany?"

"Back and forth. On the one hand, he admitted the MO for her homicide was different from the other Creekside victims, but he knew details about her case, about her back-ground...*my* background. If he didn't kill her, why would he bother collecting that information?" She dragged her knuckles across her cheek, although she hadn't shed any tears.

"It's his hobby."

"That's exactly what he said." She sniffed. "How many times have you visited him?"

He met her gaze steadily as her eyes still threw sparks at him. "I've met him three times. I recorded the conversations if you're interested in listening. It's mostly just his background, his childhood."

"Which I'm sure was terrible and delivered to induce the greatest amount of sympathy." She tossed the crushed cup onto the console.

Finn lifted his shoulders. "Single, drug-addicted mother, lots of so-called fathers in and out of his life, some of whom beat him, lots of upheaval."

"Sounds like my childhood."

A sharp pain lanced his heart. He knew all about Jessica and Tiffany's rough upbringing and how Tiffany had protected her younger sister. He understood Jessica's need for justice. He'd felt it himself.

"I'm not writing a love letter to the Creekside Killer. This is just like any other true crime book. I'll do justice to the victims and hopefully reveal what makes Plank tick. That's not an excuse for him, and it's no pity party. It's going to be a cold, hard look at a cold, hard killer."

"But your claim to fame, your raison d'être, is that you discovered the body of one of the Creekside Killer's victims—Tiffany Hunt. Without that, you're just another criminal justice expert writing a book about a serial killer. No offense."

"None taken." He ran a finger around his collar and started the rental car.

"My point being, as you do the research for this book, it's going to be in your best interests to encourage Plank to stick with his confession regarding my sister's homicide." She snapped on her seat belt and hit the dash with her palm. "Let's get out of this place."

He gritted his teeth as he pulled away from the parking space. "I don't have any best interests here, Jessica. My best interest is to write a truthful and compelling book about a killer and maybe give some dignity to the victims, including Tiffany, if Plank continues to insist he killed her. Are you beginning to believe he did?"

"I don't know." She sighed as she slumped in the passenger seat. "He reminded me of his confession while also encouraging me to compare the dissimilar MOs. I don't know what to think anymore."

"That's the way he wants it. Continue on the path you started. If you truly believe he didn't murder Tiffany and that somehow Morgan's homicide is connected to hers, then go for it. Keep investigating."

"And you'll help me?"

He felt her stare searching his profile, heard the cajoling tone of her voice, even smelled the intoxicating scent of her floral perfume that infiltrated all the sensible parts of his brain, and God help him, he was falling into her trap again.

He took a hard turn onto the highway and said, "Yeah, I'll help you. Now let's get something to drink before we get to the airport."

HOURS LATER, back in her hotel room, Jessica unzipped her boots and pulled them off, dropping each one on the carpeted floor with a clunk. She fell across the bed, and her stomach growled, the turkey sandwich in Walla Walla a distant memory.

Finn had offered to buy her dinner when they landed in Seattle and drove back to Fairwood, but she needed time away from him to digest the news about his book.

Was the book the reason he'd even agreed to look at her evidence? Despite what he said, his book would have more traction if the victim he'd discovered had actually been murdered by the subject of his book.

And was she? Jessica slid her phone from the side pocket of her purse and navigated to her recorded conversation with Plank. Finn had been right about one thing—Plank liked to play games. But he didn't scare her. It's not like he'd been wheeled out like Hannibal Lecter with a face mask. He'd behaved like any garden-variety psychopath—no remorse for his crimes or pity for his victims, elevated sense of self-worth, no sense of right and wrong.

The only time Plank had gotten under her skin was with his knowledge of Tiffany's background, of her own family. Finn had chalked it up to Plank's sick hobby. Was it his way of hinting that he had killed Tiffany?

It would be easy for her to believe him, to believe the cops, put her sister's murder behind her. She'd been close to doing just that over the past few years, but something always dragged her back into the maelstrom. This time Morgan Flemming's homicide had been the catalyst that reignited her quest for the truth.

The fact that the MO in Morgan's case mimicked Tiffany's more than either one mimicked the Creekside Killer slayings had been the strong lure.

She grabbed a pillow from the head of the bed and pulled it into her arms, where she squeezed it tightly against her chest. Had Morgan's killer counted on that? Is that why he'd left the card and the doll? Had he left them for her?

Her gaze traveled to the rag doll sitting atop the credenza, next to the TV. Nobody would've known the meaning of that rag doll except her—and she'd gotten the message loud and clear.

Time to put aside thoughts of Finn Karlsson and his stormy blue eyes. She had an investigation to pursue, and if Finn Karlsson got in the way of that investigation, she'd handle him...just like she did the last time.

THE FOLLOWING MORNING, with the rag doll tucked into a bag and a new tire on her wheel, Jessica entered Ashley King's address into her GPS. Ashley had been Tiffany's best friend at the time of the murder. They'd lived together, and Ashley had offered one of the more intriguing clues to Tiffany's murder when she told the deputies that Tiffany had sensed someone following her in the weeks leading up to her murder.

That tip didn't rule out the Creekside Killer, as Plank had been known to stalk his victims to get a sense of their routine. But he'd always snatched his victims when they were working the streets, pretending to be a mild-mannered john. Tiffany hadn't been a working girl...at the time of her homicide.

As the deputies had patiently pointed out to Jessica, Plank could've scoped out Tiffany months before the murder when she *had* been a sex worker. Plank was known to play the long game with his prey.

Fifteen minutes later, Jessica pulled into the mobile home park where Ashley lived. Jessica hadn't called first, hadn't notified Ashley that she was dropping by for a visit.

Ten years ago, Ashley's sympathy for Jessica had waned in direct proportion to Jessica's hounding of Ashley about details she didn't have. She didn't want to give Ashley a chance now to avoid her. She couldn't exactly use her position with the Washington State Patrol to demand that Ashley speak to her or answer any of her questions. Jessica had one foot in the crime lab as part of the official investigation into Morgan Flemming's murder and one foot on her own turf, reinvestigating Tiffany's murder.

Her car crawled past the mobile homes in the community until she found Ashley's number, and she swung a U-turn to park in front. She grabbed her purse and the doll and shoved her door open with her foot. She inhaled the pine scent as she slammed her car door and crunched across the gravel to the double-wide.

The long weeds in the yard stirred as she walked past them, and a profusion of flowers bowed their heads. Someone had made an attempt to spruce up the appearance of the unit, but the upkeep had outpaced them.

She rapped on the screen door, and the ripped mesh flapped back and forth. The door squeaked on its hinges as it opened, and Ashley King stared at Jessica for a second or two before recognition flooded her face.

"Oh my God. It's Jessie." Ashley kicked open the screen door so hard, Jessica had to dodge it.

In an instant, she found herself wrapped in Ashley's chubby arms, enveloped by the skunky scent of weed. "I'd recognize you anywhere—tall, blonde and fierce. At least you're still tall and blonde. How about it? You still got that chip on your shoulder?"

Jessica patted Ashley on the back. "I hope not. God, I must've been insufferable."

"Nah, just grieving hard." She cupped Jessica's face with her soft palm. "Come on in. I can't say I'm any better at keeping house than I was when me and Tiff were roomies."

"I'm not here to do an inspection," Jessica said, as she immediately scanned the room with its topsy-turvy pillows, cluttered coffee table, sporting full ashtrays and the requisite pizza box. "Looks about the same as the place you shared with Tiffany."

"Old habits die hard." Ashley grabbed a handful of papers from a cushion on the couch and dropped them on the kitchen table, already a repository for some kind of helter-skelter filing system. "Have a seat, Jessie. I heard you're a hotshot CSI lady or something."

Perching on the edge of the sagging floral couch, Jessica shrugged. "I work in a forensics lab for the state."

"I figured you'd end up doing something like that." Ashley reached for a pack of cigarettes and then pushed them between the cushions. "That or become a cop. Is that why you're in town? That poor little Morgan Flemming?"

Jessica's spine stiffened. Ashley knew she worked for the Washington State Patrol, knew about Morgan's murder and knew she was here in an official capacity. Fairwood always had a small-town vibe. Everyone must know.

"That's my official reason for being here, but you had to have noticed the similarity between Morgan's death and Tiffany's, Ashley, just like I did."

"Listen, sweetie. I loved Tiff, me and her—" she crossed one finger over the other "—two of a kind, but it didn't cross my mind that Morgan's killing was the same as Tiff's. Two murdered girls. It happens."

"I suppose you're right, but I did find something strange at the memorial site for Morgan and I wanted to ask you about it." As she reached into the bag with the doll, a man coughed from the back of the mobile home.

Her fingers curled around the rag doll, and she froze. "I'm sorry. I didn't realize you lived with someone here."

Ashley's smooth, full face flushed pink. "Well, yeah…"

"Baby, who you talking to?" A skinny guy with dirty-blond hair brushing his shoulders stepped into the living room, blinking. "Hey, it's little Jessie."

"Denny?" Jessica's mouth fell open, as her gaze darted toward Ashley, now beet-red and fidgeting. "You live here? I tried to find you, too, but couldn't get an address for you."

"I'm driving a truck. On the road most of the time, but I stay here when I'm in Fairwood." He jerked a thumb at Ashley, his nails bitten to the quick. "Me and her hooked up after…you know, after Tiff passed. Nothing bad about it, Jessie. It's like we kinda needed each other."

"I'm not judging you—either of you."

"The cops were quick to jump on me. I guess the husband and boyfriend are always prime suspects."

"It was more than that, Denny." Ashley twisted her hands in her lap. "You were dealing."

Jessica jerked her head toward Denny. How had she not known that at the time? "You were dealing drugs?"

Denny's nostrils flared as he glanced at Ashley. "Small-time stuff. Not like I was with a cartel or anything."

Jessica licked her lips. "Well, even small dealers eventually answer to the cartels, even if you're many levels removed. Why did the cops find that significant? Did you have any disgruntled customers?"

"Nothing like that, and if they were mad about something, they'd take it out on me, not my girl. Tiff had nothing to do with any of my business." He ran a hand through his scraggly hair. "I felt guilty when Tiff was murdered, but not because I had anything to do with it or brought it down on her. Just 'cuz I couldn't protect her."

Jessica's nose tingled, and her throat felt thick. "I'm sure the cops investigated that angle."

"They got their guy, anyway." Denny scratched his goatee. "It was that Creekside Killer dude, Avery Plank."

Biting her bottom lip, Ashley sent Jessica an imploring look. Ashley knew Jessica had her doubts back then, and she did, too, but she wasn't here to stir up any more anguish for Denny.

Jessica took a deep breath. "Yeah, Plank. But I came by to ask you about a doll that Tiffany had, Ashley."

"You don't even have to tell me." Ashley waved a hand in the air. "I know what you're talking about—that rag doll. Tiff told me it had sentimental value."

"This one." Jessica pulled the doll out of the bag and shook it in the air.

"Just like that doll. Did you have one as a kid, too?" Ashley shoved her hand between the cushions to retrieve the pack of cigarettes.

"I-I think this is the same doll that Tiffany had. It was mine, and I gave it to her. There was only one doll."

Ashley dropped the cigarettes. "Where'd you get that, Jessie?"

Jessica smoothed out the doll's checkered dress. Should she tell them? Would they think she was crazy? Did it matter? "I found it at Morgan Flemming's memorial, along with the flowers and candles and stuffed bears."

"That ain't possible, Jessie." Denny shook his head. "Might look like it, but that can't be the same doll. I mean, it doesn't make sense."

"Why are you so sure?"

Denny leveled his finger at the toy in Jessica's lap. "'Cuz that doll was stolen from Tiff's apartment about two weeks before the murder."

Chapter Six

Jessica's gaze tracked back to the doll, hoping to find some answers in its unblinking button eye. "Did you report it to the police?"

"The police?" Ashley stroked a cigarette she'd hastily plucked from the pack. "Jessie, it was just a doll. No offense, but I didn't like the thing anyway. Gave me the creeps. I figured one of our friends took it as a joke or one of Denny's high-as-a-kite friends snatched it. There was a guy hanging around Tiff at the time, but he left before the murder."

"I meant after the murder. Did you report the theft to the police after Tiffany turned up dead?" Jessica eyed the cigarette. A few more minutes with these two and she just might snatch it from Ashley and smoke it herself.

"Honestly—" Ashley held up her hand as if swearing in court "—I forgot all about it. It's not like someone broke in and burglarized us. Tiff mentioned it one day, and I shrugged it off."

"But someone could've broken in to take it." She glanced at Denny, who yawned and rubbed his eyes. He'd already checked out. "Denny, did you mention the theft of the doll to the cops?"

"I didn't even know it was gone, Jessie. What's the big deal about it? Somebody left a rag doll for Morgan that looks like one Tiff had."

"You don't get it." She shook the doll by the torso, and its legs and arms flopped in the air. "This is the same doll. The exact same doll that was stolen from Tiffany two weeks before she was murdered, same missing eye and everything."

Ashley and Denny exchanged a look, as if wondering when to call in the little men with the white jackets. Jessica closed her eyes and stuffed the doll back in the bag. "I suppose you wouldn't know anything about a sympathy card left at the site that mentioned Tiffany, either, right?"

"Look, Jessie." Ashley scooted toward her on the couch and hung an arm around her shoulders. "I know you loved your sister, and you were the world to Tiff, but she's gone, honey. Plank is behind bars, and you got a chance to help another murder victim now."

"She's right, Jessie." Denny stroked his goatee. "If we hear anything weird about Morgan's murder, we'll call you. Right, babe? Put Jessie's number in your phone."

After exchanging numbers with Ashley and hugging her sister's two best friends, Jessica stepped outside and took a deep breath of the fresh pine. Was she losing it? Was the rag doll just the same type of doll that happened to be missing the same eye on her face? Had the same ribbons? The same yellow yarn hair?

As she stepped up to her car, her cell phone rang. She swallowed hard as she saw her supervisor's name on the display. "Hey, Michael."

"Hi, Jessica. Are you coming to the lab today? I expected your report by today on all the physical evidence collected at the Morgan Flemming crime scene. How'd the meeting go with the sheriff's department?"

"Uh…" She slid into her car and slammed the door "I haven't had that meeting, yet, Michael."

She squeezed her eyes closed, waiting for the explosion. The silence was worse. "Are you still there?"

He cleared his throat. He'd mellowed a lot since getting custody of his daughter. "Is the sheriff's department giving you the runaround?"

"No, it's me." She started the engine and powered down the window to get some air. "I-I found some interesting items at the scene, at the memorial set up for Morgan. I sort of went off on a tangent, but I'll schedule that meeting for today, if possible, and I can transport the material evidence to the lab tomorrow."

"What *interesting items* did you find?"

"A condolence card that mentioned… Tiffany Hunt."

"Someone left a card referencing your sister?"

"Yeah, weird, huh?" She chewed on her bottom lip. Michael knew all about her obsession with her sister's case. He'd told her a few times it's why he believed she was so dogged when it came to analyzing the material evidence from other cases—but he wouldn't want her…compulsion to interfere with other cases.

"Have you tracked down the card yet? Found out if any local stores stock it, if anyone purchased it recently, camera footage?"

She thunked her forehead with the heel of her hand. She didn't need Michael Wilder telling her how to do her job. She should've already followed up on the card by now. "Haven't done that yet, but it's on my list."

"Too busy visiting Avery Plank?"

A breath snagged in her throat. She knew better than to ask Michael how he'd come by that information. He had connections she could only dream about. "I thought that would be a good move, as I saw my sister's name on that card."

He snorted. "Except you would've had to have scheduled that meeting with Plank way in advance of finding that card. Tell me, Jessica. Are you in Fairwood to analyze the evidence in the Morgan Flemming homicide, or are you there to continue the investigation into your sister's?"

"Both?" She pinned her shoulders against the seat back. "I mean, both. I'm here to do my job, but I can't help taking a second look at Tiffany's case."

"Then do it. As long as you get your work done, I don't care what you do on the side, Jessica."

"I'm on it. And I swear, Michael, I have a feeling about this. I think the more I dig into my sister's case, the more I'll discover about Morgan's killer." She thumped her chest with the flat of her hand. "It's instinct."

"I've always trusted your instincts. Don't let me down, and more importantly, don't let Morgan down."

As Michael hadn't demanded her presence at the lab today, Jessica rushed back to her hotel to start working on that card. Of course, the person who'd left the card could've purchased it online or in a different area, but she should've thought of tracing the card as soon as she'd found it. Her brain wasn't functioning correctly.

Michael was right. She owed it to Morgan and Morgan's family to do her job. The card wasn't only a lead on Tiffany's case, but it could lead to a clue on Morgan's, as well.

She pulled into the parking lot of her hotel, and her

phone rang again. Holding her breath, she looked at the display—not Michael checking up on her.

"Hi, Finn. How was your class this morning?"

"Good. How'd it go with Ashley?"

"Better than expected in some ways. I ran into Denny at her place."

"Denny Phelps? What was he doing there?"

"They're a thing. Apparently, they started seeing each other after Tiffany's death. I could tell Ashley was uncomfortable about it, but I don't begrudge them their happiness. I learned a few things, though."

"Do you want to tell me over dinner? I have office hours, a faculty meeting and an online meeting with my editor."

Had he just asked her out on a date? There had been so much sexual tension between them when he was a fresh cop and she was a college student looking for answers to her sister's murder, but once he realized she'd been using him to get information about the case, he'd dropped her. She'd realized at the time that he'd never believe her if she told him that it hadn't all been an act on her part. She hadn't even tried.

Now the sparks still kindled, but it was her turn to doubt. Did he have ulterior motives related to his book? Did he want to get close to her and her investigation to sabotage it?

"Jessica? Dinner? My treat."

"Sure. Yeah. I talked to my supervisor today, and he suggested I run a trace on the condolence card, which I should've already implemented. I didn't even get a chance to tell him about the doll, but I'll give you the details about that tonight. Seven?"

"I'll pick you up at your hotel."

He ended the call before she could change her mind—

not that she wanted to change it. She valued his insight, and she owed him. If he wanted fodder for his book, he could try to find it.

Back in her hotel room, she snapped on some blue gloves and removed the card from the safe in the closet. She flipped it over and studied the back.

Any store, including online ones, would carry this brand of card, but she could probably search most of the stores in Fairwood in a few afternoons. Might as well start now and fill up the time before meeting Finn for dinner.

Fifteen minutes later, she hit the first store. The clerk at the counter greeted her as she breezed through the front door of the small drugstore. She found a small slotted shelf of cards in the back near the batteries and phone chargers. Not one sympathy card peeked out from the rows of birthday cards and a smattering of early Halloween cards. People sent cards for Halloween?

The local grocery store didn't carry cards, and a T-shirt and knickknack shop featured only handmade cards from artists in the area. She bought two of those cards.

Peeking through the window of a convenience store, she spotted a rotating rack filled with cards. She stepped through the front doors and made a beeline for the rack. She spun it around until she saw a few thank-you and sympathy cards. She plucked the two sympathy cards from their spots. One glance told her they weren't the same as the one she found at Morgan's memorial, but the same greeting card company produced them. Progress.

She took the bagged card to the counter and held it out to the clerk. "Do you know if your store carried this particular card?"

The guy shoved his hair from his face and squinted at the card. "Is it back there?"

"No, but there are two from the same company. I was just wondering if this card may have been purchased here." She jiggled the plastic bag pinched between her fingertips at the clerk, as he seemed to be rapidly losing interest in her questions.

He blinked. "Do you have a receipt? Looks like it's been used. We can't take it back."

"I didn't buy it. I wanted to know—" she spun around and rolled her eyes "—never mind."

She tucked the card back in her purse and swung by the self-serve soda machine to fill up a cup with half root beer and half Diet Coke. This time the clerk smiled at her as he rang up her purchase.

When she got back to her car, she dropped her drink in the cup holder and pulled out her phone. Task one completed, task two up next.

The phone rang twice before King County Sheriff's Deputy Tomas Alvarado picked up. "Detective Alvarado."

"Detective Alvarado, this is Jessica Eller, Washington State Patrol Crime Lab."

"Hi, Jessica. You can call me Tomas. I was waiting for your call. Are you ready to transport the physical evidence to the lab? Marysville, right? Or is this going to Seattle?"

"Marysville. Seattle's all full up. I'd like to meet with you first and discuss the evidence. I also found a couple of items at Morgan Flemming's memorial site I'd like to show you."

"It's a little late for me today, but I can do tomorrow. Three at the station sound good?"

"I'll be there."

"In the meantime, to prep for the meeting I'll email you a list of the material evidence. We didn't categorize it yet. We'll leave it up to you guys, as usual."

"Perfect. You have my department email. Send it over, encrypted."

She ended the call and cupped the phone in her hands. Michael had been right. Time to focus on Morgan. If that led to new discoveries about Tiffany, she'd take it.

Shuffling through those greeting cards had taken her longer than she'd expected, so she rushed back to the hotel. She wanted to review the email from Tomas before she got ready for her...meeting with Finn.

Back in her room fifteen minutes later, Jessica peeked into her closet to see if she had anything halfway presentable to wear to dinner tonight. So far, Finn had seen her in jeans, T-shirts and hiking boots, and slacks and a blouse—hardly memorable. But this wasn't a date, so it didn't matter if he found her attractive.

It didn't matter because they had this...thing between them—chemistry, electricity, good old-fashioned lust. She'd wondered over the years if her attraction to Finn at that time had been because she needed him to get info on her sister's case. Maybe, feeling guilt about using him, she had convinced herself that she really did feel something for him.

This reacquaintance with him had pretty much put that theory to bed, which is exactly where she wanted him. She slid the closet door closed and smirked at herself in the mirror.

With her drink from the convenience store beside her open laptop, Jessica accessed her email. She scrolled past several, including one from Celine Jerome, a PI who specialized in genetic and family tracking. Jessica had decided to take up where Tiffany had left off tracking down their brother.

She clicked on the message from Tomas and opened the attachment. She expanded the file and ran a quick eye down the short list of items.

Outdoor crime scenes usually yielded less physical evidence than indoor ones, and the elements subjected that evidence to more deterioration and less reliability. They did pick up a shoe print, but how long had it been there? It could belong to anyone in that public area.

She opened her own file and began to make notes on the evidence in her own words. The method helped her process the items, especially when she hadn't been on the responding CSI team. She had to reconstruct the scene and the physical evidence in her head. She also used a program on her computer to sketch out the scene. Visiting it in person always helped.

A cigarette butt in the area held promise. A red cloth fiber that hadn't come from anything of Morgan's. A foil wrapper from a granola bar, but no prints on that. No prints on anything, including Morgan's neck. Most likely, her killer had strangled her with a piece of clothing. Necktie? Scarf? Is that where the red fiber came from? Plank had used a tie on her sister, although authorities had never found it.

Most of these items had been shipped to the forensic lab in Seattle for possible DNA sampling. Marysville did DNA, but this evidence had been fast-tracked, so the items that might contain DNA had been sent to Seattle. The lab in Marysville handled physical evidence, her department, and vehicle inspections, although no vehicles were involved in this case—that they knew of.

There was no evidence that Morgan had fought back, either. No skin cells beneath her fingernails, no bruising, broken fingers. Had she known her killer, or had he sneaked up behind her? Had he lain in wait…smoking a cigarette while he watched?

Her phone rang, and she jumped. Her gaze darted to the time, and she answered Finn's call as she hopped up from her chair. "I can't believe it's seven already."

"Ah, you're not ready. I'm here in my car. I guess I expected you'd be waiting out front."

"And I would've been, if I hadn't gotten so engrossed in my work. Do we have reservations anywhere?"

Finn coughed. "Sorry, no. Wasn't thinking a reservation kinda place, but that could change."

"No. That's fine. Give me fifteen minutes."

"Tell you what. Let's go to the restaurant down the street, near the dock. They do some decent fish and chips. I'll drive over there, have a beer and wait for you. I'll even order you a glass of white."

"Make it a beer, whatever you're having, and you're on."

She dropped the phone on her bed and stripped off her clothes on the way to the bathroom. This was feeling less like a date and more like a convenient business meeting. Good thing she'd left the sexy date-night clothes at home.

After a quick shower, Jessica pulled on a pair of jeans, a lightweight red sweater and a pair of boots with a small heel. She stroked on some mascara, added a red lip and fluffed up her hair. She grabbed her purse and a black leather bomber jacket and stopped at the mirrored closet. "Not bad for a sort of date on a tight timeline."

When she hit the front desk in the lobby, she asked the clerk, "Which direction do I take to the dock?"

"Take a left out of the parking lot, and you'll run right into it. Dockside Fish Grill?" He replied as she nodded. "Order the fish and chips."

"Will do, thanks."

She stuck to the sidewalk on one side of the street, as quite a few cars whizzed by. Hardly the romantic date night she'd envisioned, but Finn had probably felt the same way when he discovered she hadn't even been ready on time. Or maybe he'd envisioned no such thing.

Twinkling lights swaying in the breeze signaled the restaurant up ahead, and she quickened her pace. She could use a beer after the day she had, filled with more questions than answers.

She spotted Finn on the outdoor patio and climbed the wooden steps to join him under the heat lamp. He jumped up to pull out her chair.

"Too chilly for you? We can move inside, but the heat lamp helps and the air is refreshing, especially as I've been cooped up indoors all day."

"This is fine." She scooted her chair closer to the table and shrugged off her jacket. "How were your meetings?"

"Office hours are usually okay, but that one student of mine, Dermott Webb—you saw him after my class—he's kind of a fanboy. Always has a ton of questions, many designed as gotchas for me. He's testing me. Those kinds of students are tiresome. And the staff meeting?" He took a long swallow of his beer. "Even more tiresome."

A waitress pushed through the glass doors to the patio with a tray laden with a bottle of beer and a frosty mug. "I would've had it waiting for you, but I wanted to be sure you got it cold."

"Perfect. Thank you."

When she left, Jessica picked up her perfectly poured beer and raised it. "To less tiresome and less confusing days."

"I'll definitely drink to that." He clinked his bottle against her glass. "I'm sure your day was more interesting than mine. Tell me what you discovered."

"I discovered, thanks to my boss, that I'm putting my sister's old case ahead of Morgan's and doing her an injustice." She sipped her drink and touched her tongue to the foam on her lip.

"I think you can do both at the same time. What did you find out from Denny and Ashley?" He shoved a menu at her with one finger. "I'm ordering the fish and chips."

"Me, too, on the suggestion of the hotel desk clerk." She stacked the two menus, hitting the edges on the tabletop. "Did you know Denny was selling drugs at the time of Tiffany's murder?"

"I knew that, yeah." Finn wrapped his hands around his bottle, lacing his fingers. "That lead went nowhere. Denny was in good standing with his bosses. Didn't owe anyone. Nobody owed him. No skimming. No stealing."

She wrinkled her nose. "Wow, so he was a *good* drug dealer."

"Good enough not to make him…or his woman a target."

After the waitress took their orders, Jessica tilted her head. "You never told me that about him."

"Like I said, didn't play a role in Tiffany's murder." He tapped his bottle with his fingernail. "What else did you find out from those two?"

"The doll, my doll, the one I'd left with Tiffany, was stolen in the weeks prior to her murder."

His eyebrows bunched over his nose. "That's not in the case file. Nobody mentioned a break-in at her place."

"Ashley never reported it. Claims she's not sure anyone *did* break into their apartment. Noticed it missing but put it down to a prank or someone just walking off with it."

"You think Tiffany's killer stole the doll and then ten years later left it at the crime scene of another murder victim?" His gaze burned into her, and she wondered again how blue could cause so much heat.

"Y-yes." She took a gulp of her beer and patted the foam from her lip.

"You don't sound so sure now. Is that your doll or a replica?"

"With the same missing button?"

He lifted his shoulders. "It's a toy. Buttons go missing."

"Maybe—" she snapped her fingers three times "—it's not the same doll but one meant to look like mine."

"That brings us back to the same place. Someone ten years ago took Tiffany's doll, maybe lost it, or maybe just took notice of the doll and copied it to leave it at Morgan's memorial site. Why?"

The waitress saved her from coming up with an answer, placing their baskets of food on the table. "Anything else? Another round?"

Jessica glanced at her half-full glass and shook her head, and Finn asked for some vinegar.

The appearance of the food didn't deter him, even as he shook his napkin into his lap and picked up a french fry. He waved it at her. "Why would someone be playing you like this? How would that person even know you'd be back here?"

"I don't know. He could know my job, know I'd be on the scene for the evidence."

"Or it could have nothing to do with you at all. I think I told you before, could be a sick joke, someone fascinated with your sister's case. We both know there are people out there like that. True crime podcasts flourish, websites dig into cases new and cold. Lotta crime buffs out there. It's not a stretch to imagine that several of these fans are sickos. They want to insert themselves into cases." Finn sprinkled his fish and chips with the vinegar the waitress had left. "I'm sure it wouldn't surprise you to learn that several women have proposed to Avery Plank."

She picked up a piece of fish with her fingers and blew on it. "Don't ruin my appetite."

"I'm just sayin'." He held out the bottle of vinegar to her, and she shook her head. "Any luck with the condolence card? I'm figuring you would've led with that if you had gotten lucky."

"Exactly. Found some cards from the same company but not this particular one."

"Did you check the university's bookstore?"

"Good call." She smothered her fries with ketchup, noting Finn's horrified expression. "You know for sure the store carries cards? Do students even buy cards?"

"I know for sure you just made a mess out of your fries, but yeah. I've bought a few cards there myself. In fact, I'd hazard a guess that the majority of the students who left cards at Morgan's memorial bought them at the student store."

"I'll check tomorrow." Her phone buzzed in the side pocket of her purse, and she pulled it free, cupping it in her hand beneath the table. She squinted at the unknown number on her display and tapped it, leaving a smudge of ketchup on the screen.

Her pulse jumped as she read the message: If you wanna know what happened to ur sister meet me at morgans at 9 come alone.

She shoved the phone back in her purse and curled her fingers around the handle of her beer mug so tightly she felt as if she could snap it off.

"Everything okay?" Finn crunched into a piece of fish and raised his brows.

"That was my boss, Michael. He's not very happy with me right now and wants my evidence report like yesterday." She took a sip of beer to soothe her dry throat. "I'd started it before dinner. That's why I hadn't realized how fast the time had gone and that you were downstairs waiting for me. I hadn't even taken a shower."

She put down her beer and shoved a piece of fish in her mouth. *Stop talking, Jessica.*

"Oh, wow. Sorry. I didn't realize you were so busy. You could've canceled."

"Even overworked, overwhelmed CSIs need to eat." She flashed him a fake smile as her brain tripped out. "But I should really get back. I'll take the rest of my food with me. Do you mind?"

"Absolutely not. I'll grab a couple of to-go boxes."

As Finn left the patio, Jessica retrieved her phone and answered the unknown texter that she'd be there at nine. She knew he'd meant Morgan's memorial site, and she had every intention of being there—alone.

Chapter Seven

Finn ducked behind a potted plant and peered at the patio between its leaves, watching Jessica dip her head as she texted on her phone. Unless her boss had just threatened to fire her, he didn't believe her for one minute.

She'd actually gotten worse at lying over the years, or maybe he'd just gotten over being the besotted fool who believed everything she said. He pivoted and made a beeline toward the bar. Correction. He was still besotted but no longer a fool.

He asked for a couple of containers and a plastic bag, and catching the waitress as she ordered some drinks at the bar, he requested the check.

He took care of the bill and returned to the patio, handing a container to Jessica. "You wanna add more ketchup to those fries before boxing them up?"

"No." She didn't even crack a smile, but he noticed she'd finished off her beer. For courage?

He'd eaten more than she had and elected to leave his food on his plate. "At least I can give you a ride back to the hotel."

"That was my fault for being late. The walk wasn't bad, though." She slid her to-go box in the plastic bag and grabbed her purse. "Ready."

He was ready, too.

As she sat beside him in the passenger seat, her knees bounced, jiggling the plastic bag on her lap.

He knew not to ask questions. Better to pretend everything was normal. Better to make her believe he hadn't noticed that text had turned her world upside down. Maybe Denny and Ashley had a change of heart and were ready to spill some secrets.

The drive took less than five minutes, and he pulled up in front of the lobby. "Walk you up?"

"No. I'm sorry. I really need to get busy and finish this report tonight. Thanks for dinner." She patted the plastic bag. "And now I have a midnight snack."

"Let's touch base tomorrow. I can have a look at the card section at the student store, as I'll be on campus anyway."

"That would be great."

She couldn't get out of his car fast enough and slammed the door so hard it made the vehicle shudder. Holding up one hand in a wave, she disappeared into the hotel.

He put the car in gear and rolled around to the side of the hotel, facing the water. This gave him a clear view of the guest parking lot, and he'd already spotted her Subaru. He couldn't listen in on any phone calls she might make or see any texts, but if she planned a late-night rendezvous with Denny and Ashley, he'd see her leave.

He cut the lights and slumped in his seat. He felt as if he were on a stakeout again. Too bad he hadn't taken a coffee for the road. Finn turned on the radio and watched a few people come and go from dinner, headlights training in and out of the parking lot.

When a lone figure darted from the hotel into the parking lot, he sat up. The lights on Jessica's car flashed as she scurried toward it.

Finn started his engine but left his headlights off. If stopped, he knew enough officers on the force that they might let him get away without a ticket. There wasn't enough traffic on the road for Jessica not to notice a single car following her. He'd have to use all his forgotten surveillance skills for this one.

As she pulled out of the parking lot, he trailed after her, allowing another car to get between them. Hanging back, he duplicated her turns away from the pier toward the university. For a minute, he expected her to turn into the campus. Maybe she'd just decided to check out the student store on her own.

Then she turned left onto the road that bordered the university—and led to the forest trail. Was she actually going there? And why?

He made the same turn but slowed down, as he'd lost the car in the middle blocking her view of his vehicle. She couldn't turn off many places along this route. This road eventually led to the coast, but she wouldn't have taken the long way around to get there.

When her brake lights flashed ahead, he hung back even more. Had she spotted him in her rearview? Not that she shouldn't be watching her back after that tire stunt.

Finn let out a breath when she picked up speed, and he accelerated to follow. His Jeep sat too high to be overlooked, and even with his lights out, a watchful eye would be able to detect his approach. He'd have to slow down, let her get well ahead and just hope he'd see her car parked at the side or in a pullout.

He also hoped he'd get there in time to save her—from what, he didn't know, maybe just from herself.

JESSICA STEERED HER car into the pullout that would give her access to the trail leading to Morgan's memorial site. Is this where her killer had parked? Or had he been stealthier, coming from a direction where no one would notice him?

The CSIs on the scene had checked this pullout for tire tracks, but there had been too many to distinguish one set. They hadn't had any better luck with the area across the river. Too many people used this trail, although nobody had witnessed a man in the area. One couple had passed Morgan on the trail, probably less than fifteen minutes before she'd been murdered.

Jessica gave a little shiver and slid her Sig into her pocket. She might be taking her life in her hands by agreeing to meet a stranger at the site of two murders, but she was going to have a gun in at least one of those hands while she did it. The texter had said come alone, not come unarmed and defenseless.

She eased from her car and snapped the door closed. She'd leave it unlocked in case she needed to make a quick getaway. Before diving into the woods, Jessica glanced over her shoulder. A few sets of headlights had been behind her up until the university, and she thought she'd seen a shadow behind her on the road out here, but that didn't make sense.

Whoever had invited her was probably already in place waiting for her. She dipped her hand into her pocket and wrapped her fingers around the handle of her weapon. The hiking boots she'd swapped in for the low heels she'd worn at dinner crunched through the forest floor. She didn't try to conceal her presence. She didn't want to startle the guy.

This could be another prank, but she couldn't risk not knowing. If someone had information about her sister's murder, well, that's what she was looking for. A little danger wasn't going to deter her.

She strode toward Morgan's memorial, which had grown since the last time she and Finn had found the rag doll here. Her classmates wanted to pay their respects, maybe even pressure the police, who didn't seem to have much to go on right now—and she should know given that paltry evidence list. Something else was going to have to crack this case—and she just might hold the key.

She called out. "Hello? It's Jessica Eller. Tell me what you know. Show your face."

A rustling noise beyond the trees answered her, and she spun toward it. "This is your meeting. I'm here. Tell me what you got. What do you know about Tiffany?"

Whispering filtered through the cedars and the red alders, their branches still full from summer and bulking up for the winter, but Jessica couldn't tell if it was a human voice or the sound of the leaves playing tricks on her willing mind. "Hello?"

A crunch of sticks and a crackle of twigs vibrated through the air, the rhythmic sound an echoing of footsteps on the trail. Was he running away from her? Had she scared him away with her bold approach?

Putting her head down, she used her arms to swim through the foliage at the edge of the clearing, stumbling on the path next to the creek. She tipped her nose to the sky like an animal catching a scent from the breeze and held her breath. Beyond her thundering heart, she heard the footsteps traipsing through the forest, the littered ground beneath his feet pinpointing his direction.

She veered to the right, and clutched a stitch in her side as she took the path to her sister's murder site. Was he playing some cruel game with her? Did he want her to follow him? He didn't seem to be doing anything to conceal his tread.

"I'm coming. I'm following you." She panted the words, more out of apprehension than any physical exhaustion.

Still, he remained ahead of her, teasing her, goading her, leading her to the one place in the world that had the power to break her. And he knew it.

She stumbled to a stop at a place where the creek gurgled louder and where a twisted branch reached out from the water to grab her. She dropped to her knees, the pebbles gouging the flesh beneath her jeans.

A sob bubbled in her throat. She choked out, "I'm here. Is this where you want me? Tell me what you know."

Sitting back on her heels, she ran her arm beneath her nose, her gaze scanning the area. What did he want? The footsteps, louder now to compensate for the rushing water, stomped ahead. He wasn't finished with her yet.

She scrambled to her feet and lurched forward, like a drunk craving one more drink, even though he knew he'd had enough. Even though he knew nothing good lay ahead.

Adrenaline raced through her body now, and her legs pumped faster and with more assurance. She'd catch him. She'd catch him if it was the last thing she did this night. She plowed ahead with purpose, her jaw clamped, her breathing heavy through her nose.

When she heard the laugh, she froze. The high-pitched sound sent rivers of ice down her back. She pulled the gun from her pocket, her itching finger on the trigger.

She crept forward more slowly. "What's so funny? Why don't you show me what's so funny?"

She took a few steps, stopped and listened. Took a few more steps, stopped and listened. Nothing. The owner of that hair-raising laugh had stopped moving, stopped communicating with her.

"Jesssssica."

Had that been the breeze breathing her name? She cranked her head toward the creek and jerked back. Hunching forward, Jessica inched close to the water's edge.

Then she clapped a hand to her mouth, but it didn't do any good. A scream ripped through her throat as the eyes of a dead girl stared back at her.

Chapter Eight

Finn dug the heels of his tennis shoes into the dirt and eyed the pile of stuffed animals, candles and flowers, balloons floating above it all. From his position, he did a three-sixty but didn't see any sign of Jessica.

The location of her car on the road indicated she'd come to Morgan's memorial, as they'd parked there when they were here together. Why would she go anywhere else? Unless someone took her against her will.

Crouching down, he used the flashlight from his phone to scan the ground, looking for a disturbance or signs of a struggle. But he was no professional tracker, and the sticks, leaves, pebbles and other detritus from the forest littered the ground in the haphazard pattern he'd expect.

He glanced up, taking in the trail that led through the trees to the edge of the creek. She didn't get it in her head to take a stroll past her sister's murder site, did she? What would possess her to do that? Unless it wasn't her idea.

His heart thumped as he pushed to his feet and strode toward the path to the creek. Before he even got there, a woman's scream ripped through the night air.

The hair on the back of his neck stood on end, and his feet started moving in the direction of the sound. The shriek had set the whole forest in motion. Creatures scurried around him under cover of the darkness and underbrush, and birds took flight, twittering and flapping.

Once he swallowed his shock and got his breath back, he shouted. "Jessica! Jessica!"

The critters responded to his intrusion with more chirping and rustling, but humans had other ways of communicating. Without missing a step, Finn pulled out his phone and called Jessica.

His chest heaved and his vision blurred as her phone rang. When he finally heard her voice on the other end, he staggered to a stop. "Jessica?"

Her reply, breathless and hoarse, almost took him to his knees in relief. "Oh my God. Finn, there's another one. There's another dead woman."

Goose bumps marched across his flesh as he clutched the phone, trying to keep Jessica close. "I'm here in the forest. I heard your scream. I'm by the creek, just past the crime scene."

"Keep following the waterline. Go past Tiffany's murder site for several more yards. I-I'm here. There's a body by the water."

He started jogging, phone plastered to his ear. "Stay on the line with me. I'm almost there. We'll call 911 when I reach you. Are you safe?"

"The killer's gone, if that's what you mean, and I have my Sig Sauer by my side."

"Thatta girl. Keep it handy, but I'm coming at you in about a minute. Don't shoot me."

When he came around the last bend in the creek, he ended the call with Jessica and shone his flashlight on her standing beside a crumpled form at the water's edge, her weapon in her hand at her side. His gut twisted in knots. He'd been so focused on getting to Jessica, he hadn't let the news of another body sink in—until now.

His stride ate up the final feet between them, and he pulled her against his chest with one arm. Her body trembled against him. "God, I'm glad you're okay."

"I am—" she sniffled and pointed her gun at the body "—but she's not."

"Have you touched the body? Done any kind of observation?"

"Just checked her pulse to make sure she didn't have any life left to save. Sh-she was still warm. I didn't want to touch anything else." She wriggled from his grasp and tapped her phone. "I'm calling it in."

He didn't want to touch anything, either, but he crouched beside the young woman, her eyes staring, her black hair spread out in a fan behind her head, and ran his light around her face and neck. The redness around her throat indicated another strangling. Small scratches marred her skin, and he directed his light to her hand resting across her chest. One broken fingernail and a few drops of blood indicated this poor girl had fought to breathe, fought to remove the object around her neck, strangling the life out of her.

Finished with her call to 911, Jessica nudged him in the back with her toe. "Careful."

He rose beside her. "Strangled, probably with a tie or scarf. Most likely not a rope or wire."

"Just like Morgan—" Jessica rubbed her upper arms "—and Tiffany, but *not* like the other Creekside victims."

"Well, we know where Avery Plank is, so it's definitely not him." Finn stepped away from the body, pulling Jessica with him. "What were you doing out here? How'd you find this body?"

"What were *you* doing out here?"

"I followed you." He shrugged, not ashamed of his actions. "After you got that text at dinner, you seemed off. I figured you were up to something and if you didn't want to tell me, it was probably something you knew you shouldn't be doing."

"What are you, the hall monitor?" She narrowed her eyes, but he didn't flinch.

"You're welcome. I may have saved your life."

"It's not my life that needed saving."

"Are you going to tell me what happened or make me find out when you talk to the police because I *know* you're not lying to them." He crossed his arms and puffed out his chest, even though he really wanted her back in his embrace. For all her tough talk, her eyes looked glassy in the darkness, and that scream still echoed in his brain.

"I got a text from someone who told me to meet him at Morgan's memorial site if I wanted to find out what happened to Tiffany."

Anger fizzed in his veins, and he wanted to berate her for her carelessness—but that wasn't the way to get Jessica Eller to talk. "Unknown number, I presume."

"You presume correctly, and we can further presume that any tracing of the number is going to come back to a burner phone, but I'm still going to run a trace."

"Okay." He curled his fingers into his biceps. "Morgan's memorial site. I was there. You weren't. What happened from there?"

"I stopped there for a few minutes waiting, and then I

began to hear noises in the woods—human noises. Footsteps."

"Someone out there just stomping around after committing a murder."

"No stealthy creeping. He definitely wanted me to hear him…and follow him." She rubbed her hands together in front of her, as if trying to get warm even though she still wore the jacket from dinner.

"Follow him?"

"His footsteps were quite clear. Every time I stopped to listen, he'd respond by leading me on with his footsteps. Once I started along the path, it became clear that he was leading me to Tiffany's crime scene." She covered her mouth with her hand.

"You got to…that location and then what happened?"

Her eyes widened as she reached out and grabbed his arm. "He laughed."

"Laughed? What kind of laugh?" Finn clenched his jaw. What kind of evil laughed after committing a murder? Avery Plank for one, and there were many others.

"A horrible, high-pitched laugh." Jessica covered her ears as if she could still hear it. She probably could.

"I think it came from across the creek. He must've come from the other side. The deputies need to check that access road for tire tracks. I know they did for Morgan's murder, too, but this time they might be able to discern fresh tracks. I never did hear a car. Did you?"

"I didn't hear a car. Didn't hear a laugh, either." He chewed on his bottom lip. "After you screamed, did you hear me calling your name?"

"No. I just got your call, which stunned me for a few seconds. Of course, I didn't have any idea when I saw the call

come through that you were actually in the forest with me."
She gave him a sideways glance. "I'm glad you were here."

"Me, too, but that means the killer probably didn't hear
me yelling, either. So he didn't know I was here."

"I think he left after I screamed. He left once he made
sure I'd found his handiwork." She pointed down the path
that led to another entrance to the trail. "Sirens."

"If he didn't hear me, didn't know I was out here, I probably didn't save your life."

"You sound disappointed." She shoved her hands in the
front pockets of her jeans and screwed up one side of her
mouth.

"No, no. I'm relieved you weren't in physical danger."
He stepped toward the water, making a wide berth around
the dead woman, and stared at the other side of the creek.
"I'm just wondering why. What does he want with you?
Why lead you to another dead body?"

"It's clear to me." She raised her arms in the air, cell
phone flashlight clasped in one hand, and waved at the
deputies charging up the trail. "He either killed Tiffany
or knows who did. He's playing a game with me…and I'm
all in."

ABOUT TWO HOURS later at the stroke of midnight, Jessica
kicked her feet in the chilly water and took another sip of
beer from the bottle she and Finn had bought at the little market inside her hotel. Her shoulder bumped his as
they sat side by side at the edge of a small mooring area
outside the hotel. After the deputies had grilled them—or
rather grilled *her*, Finn's buddies on the force had *questioned* him—they'd been too pumped up to go their separate ways and call it a night. What a night.

Tapping her knee, he said, "Your toes are going to freeze in that water."

"Then they'll match the rest of me. I'm not over the shock of finding Missy Park. Why weren't the deputies patrolling that trail after Morgan's murder? And what was Missy doing there by herself?"

Finn tipped back his bottle, took a long swallow and slammed it down on the wooden slats of the dock. "I could ask you the same question."

She caught her breath. She knew Finn would be angry about it. Knew he'd try to talk her out of it. That's why she'd hidden it from him. She said, lightly, "Asked and answered."

"If a stranger texted you to go jump off the Space Needle, would you do that, too?" He collapsed on his back, folding his arms beneath his head.

"I would do a lot to solve my sister's murder. I owe it to her." She glanced at his bunching biceps, his T-shirt stretched across the hard planes of his chest. The boy had become a man—a harder, less forgiving one, a less malleable one.

He turned his head. "Do you think Tiffany would want you to put yourself in danger to find her killer? Tiffany protected you. You told me yourself she risked her life to protect you when you were children. She'd want you to live your life, Jessica."

"If the drunk driver that killed your father while he was on patrol hadn't been apprehended at the scene, are you telling me you wouldn't have moved heaven and earth to find that person and bring him to justice? You know you would have. You went into a career that you didn't even like just to honor his memory."

Finn closed his eyes, and she reached out and stroked his

thigh. "I'm sorry to bring that up…but you know it's true, Finn. I never believed the Creekside Killer was responsible for Tiffany's death. It didn't add up to me. Avery Plank never stalked his victims. His were crimes of opportunity. He picked up sex workers and dumped them on trails, at campsites, recreational areas. Tiffany's killer stalked her."

"You know the theory." He rolled onto his side and propped up his head with his hand, his elbow planted on the wooden dock.

"That Plank knew her when she'd been turning tricks, discovered her again and decided to kill her." She flipped her hand in the air. "Nope. Tiffany wouldn't have met up with a former john. I doubt she'd even remember him. This person stalked her, perhaps stole the rag doll and slipped away when Plank took the blame."

"Never to strike again. You don't have to take one of my classes to know how unlikely that is—especially if this killer was unknown to Tiffany."

"I've thought of that. He could've gotten picked up for another crime. He didn't leave any DNA at Tiffany's scene. Didn't sexually assault her, probably for that same reason. If the cops had picked him up for peeping or burglary or assault, they wouldn't have had any DNA to match him up with Tiffany's murder."

"So, he's been in jail for the past ten years and decided to come back to the scene of his first murder and start up again—while contacting the sister of his victim."

"Yeah, I don't know." She pulled her feet from the water and curled her legs beneath her. "I'm just so heartbroken for Missy and Morgan. I wonder if the investigators will find any connection between the two women other than the first letter of their first names and the fact that they were both on that trail at night. Just like Morgan, Missy was wearing running clothes and earbuds. So it would seem they were both on that trail voluntarily. Why would Missy go running where another woman had been murdered just a week before?"

"People do careless things all the time." He sat up and gave her a hard stare. "Are you going back to the crime scene in the morning when it's light out to finish your examination?"

"Yeah, poor Deputy Holden has to spend the night out there to guard it. I'm not the only CSI member who's going back. We still need to look for tracks. Also, I told Detective Morse that I'm pretty sure the killer had been farther up the trail at Morgan's site. He could've left pieces of evidence along that trail without realizing what he was doing." She stuck her legs out in front of her and wiggled her toes as she grabbed one of her socks. "He was sloppy this time."

"I hope Missy got his DNA beneath her fingernails. I saw blood. Of course, it could be her own blood, as I also saw scratches on her neck. The poor girl was probably trying to claw the scarf from her neck as he twisted it tighter and tighter."

Jessica swallowed, the beer tasting bitter on the back of her tongue. "How do you know it's a scarf and not a tie or a sleeve or something else?"

"I don't. Just a guess." He smacked both hands on the dock and pushed up to his feet. "Let's get going before your toes turn to icicles."

She shoved her feet into her hiking boots. "Warm and cozy now."

He hovered over her, extending his hand. She took the offer, and he pulled her up beside him. He kept hold of her hand and with the other brushed a lock of hair from her forehead. "I was scared as hell when I heard you scream. That few seconds before you answered your phone felt like minutes ticking by in my head while I imagined all sorts of things happening to you."

"Instead of screaming, I should've gone after him. I had my gun. I knew he'd cross the creek. I could tell from his creepy laugh. Maybe I could've…caught him. Stopped him."

He pinched her chin, his thumb almost touching her bottom lip. She closed her eyes, waiting for his anger to well up again, waiting for him to chastise her for her stupidity.

His lips brushed hers, and her eyes flew open. The tenderness that touch communicated melted the ball of fear and tension lodged in her chest, replaced by a deep longing. Before she could respond in kind, because oh, she did want to kiss him back, he drew away from her.

His voice rough, he said, "I'm glad you didn't."

Lacing his fingers with hers, he tugged her back up the dock toward the hotel. They dropped their beer bottles into the trash can in the parking lot, and he finally released her hand as they stood just inside the lobby.

She wanted to invite him up to her room, but that desire felt so wrong hours after discovering Missy Park crumpled at the side of the creek.

He made the decision for them as he turned toward the door. "Try to get some sleep. You'll have a busy day tomorrow, and school is going to be a nightmare again. I haven't forgotten about the card. I'll have a look in the student store."

"Thanks again for…following me. See, you've still got those instincts."

He made a gun with his fingers and cocked it at her before heading back to his car.

She sighed as she crossed the lobby, and the hotel clerk called out to her. "Did you hear about another body down by the creek? Just like Morgan."

"I did. Terrible news."

"Be safe out there, Ms. Eller."

"Oh, I will." She patted the gun in her pocket on the way to the elevator. She'd be safe enough from physical danger, but keeping her heart safe from Finn Karlsson was another matter.

Chapter Nine

The following morning, Finn still had that kiss on his mind. He hadn't wanted to take advantage of the situation, as Jessica had been shaken up by the discovery of Missy Park's body.

What kind of sick game was this guy playing with Jessica? Why her? If he didn't kill Tiffany Hunt ten years ago, he was obviously fascinated with the case, seeking to make Jessica a part of these current murders.

Finn could no longer ignore the fact that the person tormenting Jessica had killed Morgan and Missy. He had led Jessica right to his most recent trophy. That was no coincidence—he'd wanted her to find Missy's body.

Finn knew the investigators were already trying to trace the number that texted Jessica last night. She'd turned over her cell phone to them at the scene, but she'd nailed it. The number would belong to an untraceable burner phone.

Finn hoped they'd find some useful evidence at the scene. If the killer led Jessica on from Morgan's murder site to Missy's, he may have left a trail.

Finn still had his contacts at the King County Sheriff's Department where his father had worked as a deputy for fifteen years. That's why the department had asked him to stand with them when Detective Morse held an information meeting for the students this morning. A sense of dread had crept over Finn as he had stared out at worried, fearful faces, many of them past and present students.

He hit the lights and locked up as he left his office. He had his own piece of the investigation to do today.

In the university bookstore, he took the escalator up to the student store and squeezed past a gaggle of people clustered around the energy drink display.

He located the carousel of cards in the back of the store and spun it around to find the sympathy cards. As he ran his fingers down the empty racks, someone bumped his elbow.

"Sorry, Dr. Karlsson." One of his students hovered behind him, her backpack swinging in front of her. "Are you looking for a card to leave for Missy Park, too?"

"I...uh, yeah. Looks like they're all sold out."

The student, whose name he'd forgotten, dabbed the end of her nose with a tissue. "Maybe they never restocked them after Morgan's murder. My parents want me out of here. Thought I'd be safer at this small school than at U-Dub, but Seattle isn't looking so bad right now."

"They'll catch him, but in the meantime, stay safe. Don't walk alone at night, skip the online dating for now. Did you know either of the women?"

"Saw Missy once in a while because she worked at the bookstore, and I work at the coffeehouse inside the bookstore. Nice girl. Smart. Don't know why she'd be running at night alone, especially after what happened to Morgan." She gave a little shiver. "I'm not going out—I mean, except with my friends."

All these students were too trusting. "Well, take care... and get yourself some pepper spray."

The girl's eyes widened as he turned away and went to the counter, grabbing a bottle of juice on his way. When it was his turn, he leaned in and said, "How long have you been sold out of sympathy cards?"

The kid, Ryan according to his name tag, blinked and ran a hand through his curly hair. "I think for a while, Professor Karlsson. Sold out after Morgan." He looked left and right, and then leaned in and whispered, "Are you helping with the investigation?"

"Yeah." Well, wasn't he?

"I'm sure my manager can give you more info on the cards, like what we stock, when they were ordered and stuff like that. He's down in the basement, management offices, when he's not up here, riding our asses." Ryan's face colored up to the curls flopping on his forehead as he rang up the juice. "Don't tell him I said that."

"I got you. What's your manager's name?"

"Deke Macy." Ryan guffawed. "You can imagine what we call him behind his back."

"Unfortunate name." Finn slipped a twenty across the counter. "Thanks, Ryan."

Finn cracked open the juice as he walked back toward the escalators. The basement of the university bookstore housed the business end of the whole complex, which included the convenience store he'd just left, a coffeehouse, a cookies and ice cream shop, and a business center that offered printers and mailing supplies to this digital generation that didn't own anything like that.

Fewer students roamed the space down here where older professionals held down the fort. Finn cruised the perimeter until he located the management offices and pushed through the door.

A woman behind a banking type window glanced up at his entrance and pushed her glasses up into her neat Afro. "Hello, can I help you?"

"I'm Finn Karlsson over in criminology. I'm looking for Deke Macy."

"Oh, hi, Professor Karlsson. Saw you at the information meeting this morning. Terrible what's happening on this campus. I'm Nia Humphry. I run accounting down here in the bowels of the beast."

"You do an awesome job, Nia. You can call me Finn. Is Mr. Macy in?"

"You can call him Deke. He's in his office. I'll buzz you in, and you'll see his office when you make a left." She waved a hand behind her.

She buzzed the door and as he slipped through, a head popped around one of the cubicles. "Oh, hello, Dr. Karlsson."

Finn schooled his face into a pleasant smile when he saw Dermott Webb. Just his luck. The guy had better not try to corner him here with his tedious questions. "Mr. Webb. What brings you to this part of campus?"

Nia spoke up for him. "Oh, I couldn't manage without Dermott's help back here. He's a part-timer but could probably do my job."

"Not true." Dermott gave Nia a shy smile. "I have some inventory and accounting background from my stint in the army, so I jumped when I saw this job advertised."

"Well, I'm glad you did, baby. Show Professor Karlsson Deke's office."

"This way, Dr. Karlsson."

Finn followed Dermott's stiff back down a short hallway lined with small offices. The dude must be better with numbers than people.

Dermott stopped and pointed but didn't go near the doorway himself. He mouthed, *this one*.

Finn poked his head inside the office as he tapped on the door. "Deke?"

Deke dragged his gaze away from the computer monitor in front of him and gave Finn the once-over. "Yeah. Who wants to know?"

"I'm Finn Karlsson, professor over in criminology. Just had a couple of questions for you about the student store inventory—if you can help me out." Finn took two steps into the small office and extended his hand to Deke across the messy desk.

Deke stood up, the fluorescent light bouncing off his perfectly shaved head, and stuck out his hand. As they shook, Deke gave Finn's hand a crushing squeeze. Obviously, those muscles he cultivated weren't just for show. He had the strength to go along with them.

"Sure, I know you. Have a seat." Deke snapped his laptop closed and leaned back in his chair, crossing his arms behind his head, biceps flexed.

Was this a contest or something? Finn kept his muscles under wraps and sat in the lone chair opposite the desk. "I was just in the student store and had a question about the sympathy cards."

Deke winked. "You helping out the cops on these murdered girls?"

"Not really. Was in the store to pick up a juice—" he held up the bottle as proof "—saw the cards and had a thought."

"Shame about those girls. Couple of hot ones, too, but if you ask me, girls shouldn't be running around campus with their skimpy workout clothes at night and not expect some attention."

Finn clenched his fist in his lap. "They got more than attention, didn't they?"

"Yeah, yeah. Horrible stuff. The parents—" he shook his bald head "—can't imagine. I got a daughter myself. My ex is a bitch, but what are you gonna do?"

Maybe not victim-blame and call women bitches for a start. Finn swallowed his retort. "Anyway, about those cards. About how many do you stock and how many did you sell after Morgan's murder? Did you sell out and restock?"

Deke flipped open his laptop again, and his fingers raced across the keyboard. "We don't stock many sympathy cards. I mean, what do college kids have to be sorry about? Let's see, Morgan Flemming was murdered eight days ago. Had a full complement of sympathy cards on that day—about twenty-five of them. Sold out of every last one two days after that. Haven't restocked yet. More coming in a few days. Who knew we'd have a run on sympathy cards?"

Finn had pulled out his phone that contained the picture of the condolence card with Tiffany's name on it, but he kept it in his lap, tracing its edges with his fingertip. Did he really want to show the card to Deke? The guy hadn't hesitated one second when coming up with the date of Morgan's murder, and he had a creepy vibe. He should probably just turn this info over to Detective Morse or Deputy Holden, Zach, his buddy from the academy.

As he shifted in his chair, a voice trilled his name from the doorway. "Oh, hey, Professor Karlsson. We're still having class tomorrow, right?"

He twisted around and greeted one of his students, Gabby Medina, tucking her long dark hair behind one ear. "Hi, Gabby. Yes, we're having class. What are you doing here? I didn't realize so many students worked on the management side of things on campus. Good experience."

She wrinkled her nose. "I don't work here. I work at the ice cream shop, but this is where we pick up and drop off the money for the registers. I saw Dermott out front and asked about class. He told me you were back here with Deke and to ask you myself."

"Hi, Gabbeeeey." Deke waved at her with his fingers as he drew out her name.

"Hi, Dick, I mean Deke." She waved at him in the same manner, rolling her eyes. "Thanks, Professor Karlsson. I'll see you in class tomorrow."

When Gabby's footsteps faded away, Deke gave Finn another wink. "Hot little number. As a professor, I bet you have all the girlies fawning over you."

Finn studied Deke through half-lidded eyes until the other man coughed and shifted his gaze back to his computer. "So, that's what we have on the cards. Anything else?"

Definitely not showing this guy the card.

Finn asked, "All the employees who work on campus come here for the register money?"

"Not all. Just the ones who open or close the register. Nia handles those transactions, along with that dork Dermott." Deke cracked his knuckles. "Anything else, Professor?"

"No, thanks for your help." He'd investigate the hell out of this guy if he still worked in that capacity—but he didn't. As he stood at the door, Finn made a half turn. "Yeah, one more thing. You could pull the transaction records for whoever bought a card, right? Or video surveillance?"

Did the skin around Deke's mouth just blanch?

"N-not the video. We record over that, but the transactions? Sure, as long as it was a card purchase and not cash."

And if Deke Macy bought any sympathy cards to leave at a memorial site, he'd know that and most assuredly pay cash.

"You've been a big help, Deke." Finn hit the doorjamb with the palm of his hand. "Thanks, man."

Before he left the management office, Finn stopped at the front window. "Nia, do you know if either Morgan Flemming or Missy Park came to this office to open or close a register? I know they both worked at the bookstore complex."

Her face creased with concern. "Did they, now? I don't recall. Dermott, you remember?"

Dermott peered around the computer monitor. "They weren't regulars, but that doesn't mean they weren't here. Sometimes the regulars are out, or they send someone else. So anyone who works in the complex could conceivably handle the money. I didn't realize they both worked on campus."

Finn could see the calculation in Dermott's eyes from here. He hoped none of his students were going to take it upon themselves to do some investigating on their own— like he was.

"Thanks, you two. Now I know where to go if I ever need change."

"You can come visit anytime you like, Dr. K."

"Thanks, Nia." He stopped one more time with one foot out the door and made a half turn.

"How long have you been working here, Nia?"

"Oh, baby." She waved a set of manicured nails in the year. "Don't age me, now. I've been here for over twenty years."

He lowered his voice. "And Deke? How long has he been working in this office?"

"This office?" Nia rolled her eyes to the ceiling. "I'd say about four years."

Finn's shoulders slumped as he widened the door. "Okay, thanks again."

"That's *this* office." She wagged a finger at him. "He's been working at the university for longer than that, maybe twelve years total."

"Really?" That stopped Finn in his tracks. So Deke was here when Tiffany was murdered. He never mentioned that murder to Finn.

"He climbed his way up the ladder. Proud of it, too. He'll tell you himself he started as a lowly food service worker."

"Food service, huh?"

Finn exited the office, chewing the side of his thumb. Hadn't Tiffany worked in food service?

Chapter Ten

"You discovered the body?" Michael's voice rumbled over the phone. "What the hell are you doing out there, Jessica?"

"The killer wanted me to discover Missy, Michael. He lured me out and led me on."

"The question is, why would you allow yourself to be lured and led by anyone? You're there to collect and analyze evidence for a murder...now two."

"I completed the evidence report on Morgan Flemming, and I'm ready to send it to you this afternoon. I just came back from my meeting with Deputy Alvarado, and I was at the Missy Park crime scene before that." She'd been enumerating her accomplishments on her fingertips—not that Michael could see her over the phone. "I'm busy, Michael, but this killer has some sort of interest in my sister's case. He's pulling me into it."

"That's dangerous. You don't need to be pulled into anything. The next time you get a text like that, you call Detective Morse." He cleared his throat, lecture over. "Any more evidence present at the Park crime scene than Morgan's?"

"A bit more. Found red fibers again, this time under Missy's fingernails, and I found more on the trail."

"The fibers could be from the murder weapon wrapped around her throat."

"That's what I'm thinking." She was also thinking about that rhyme on the sympathy card—something old, something dead, something stolen, something red She heard a beep on his end of the line.

"I have to take this call. You be careful. It sounds like someone's put a target on your back for whatever reason."

The reason was that she was Tiffany's sister. "I'll be careful."

Red fibers. Had Jessica just tripped over another coincidence? Red had been Tiffany's favorite color. She'd owned a lot of red clothing. What had her sister been wearing when she was killed?

Jessica checked the phone she'd gotten back from the sheriff's department. They'd downloaded her data and would try to trace the phone that texted her, although they all knew it wouldn't be that easy.

No messages from Finn today. Was it because he knew she didn't have her phone or because of that kiss last night? She'd been waiting for a kiss from him for a long time. When she'd been leading him on ten years ago, she hadn't wanted him to kiss her. By the time she wanted it, he'd discovered her deception and had backed off.

She'd like to think they had another chance. She scrolled through her contacts and tapped his name.

He answered on the first ring, as if he'd been waiting. "You got your phone back."

"Yes, the deputies got what they wanted and gave it back to me. I've had an exhausting day on top of that terrifying night, but I have something else to get through before I can rest."

"Can I help?"

Finn never failed her. "Do you still have the case file from my sister's murder?"

"I don't have *the* case file, but I have a ton of copies and notes. What do you need?"

She scooped in a big breath. "I want to know what my sister was wearing that night, specifically."

"I don't remember, but I know it wasn't running clothes like these two women."

Jessica gave a short laugh. "My sister in running clothes? No way. I'd like to see a catalog of her clothing, down to her socks and shoes. Do you think your files have that?"

"I'm sure they do." He paused and sipped something. "How about you come to my place tonight for dinner? I'll share the files with you—and some other information I discovered today—and you can let me know why Tiffany's clothing has become important to you."

"I'd like that, but I don't want to put you out. Do you cook?"

"Not well, but there's a great Chinese place near the university, and I can swing by there on my way home. I'm still at the school. Does that work?"

"Perfectly. What time do you want me there? And I promise I won't be late this time."

He replied, "Or sneak out to meet a killer?"

"No promises there."

They decided on a time, and he gave her directions to his place. Maybe they did have a second chance.

A few hours later, Jessica pulled her car behind Finn's Jeep and idled, taking in the view. Through the open window, the sweet, sticky smell of alder, the fresh spiciness of the pine and the salt from the bay combined to create an invigorating aroma that prickled her face. She inhaled it before rolling up the window and cutting the engine.

She strode up the stone walkway and caught glimpses of the bay undulating behind the house. A profusion of blooms spilled over flower boxes hugging the house, their colors visible but muted beneath the lights that flashed on at her approach. She almost waved at the cameras she knew Finn would have pointing at the porch.

She rang the doorbell, a bottle of white wine in a gift bag swinging from her fingertips. Did white go with Chinese? Did Finn even like white wine? She should've brought beer instead.

As she switched the bag from one hand to the other, Finn answered the door in a pair of faded jeans and a white T-shirt that clung to his muscles. He looked hot in his professor slacks and jacket but even hotter when he dressed down. He'd told her he avoided dressing casually for class because he wanted to draw that line between himself and his students—probably to fend off all the female students hot for teacher, too.

"You found me." He ushered her inside the cozy living room, decked out in warm beige and brown hues with splashes of orange and red Native American influences.

The room enveloped her in a warm hug, but the sliding glass doors to the deck in the back drew her like a magnet. She parked in front of the doors and gazed at the glassy bay beyond, a wooden pier jutting into its depths. "Is that your boat?"

"Perfect, isn't it? I can motor over to Whidbey or the San Juan Islands."

Something goosed her from behind and she squealed

and spun around. A fawn-colored Lab wagged its tail enthusiastically.

"Bodhi! I thought I taught you better manners than that." Finn lifted his hand over the dog's head. "Sit and shake."

Bodhi complied and sat at Jessica's feet, lifting one paw for the taking. She grabbed its paw. "Hello, Bodhi. Male?"

"Yeah, he's my camping, hiking, boating, fishing companion."

Scratching behind Bodhi's ear, she said, "No wonder you don't have a wife."

Finn cocked his head. "Do you have a pet?"

"I had a cat, but she died last year."

"Sorry to hear that. It's always hard losing a pet." He raised his brows. "Is that why you don't have a husband?"

"Probably reason 992." She held up the wine bag. "I brought a bottle of white. Is that okay?"

"That's fine. I bought a bottle for you, too, but yours is cold, so we'll drink this first."

"First? Are we having a second?"

"You did say it was a rough day."

He took the wine to the kitchen, and she trailed after him. The Chinese food cartons littered the countertop, and he'd set a small table with place mats, plates, silverware and wineglasses.

"You could've just hidden the evidence and pretended you'd cooked this feast yourself." She swept a hand across the counter. "I would've never known and been so impressed."

"Never had you pegged as a woman impressed by food or cooking or…lying." He picked up one of the white plastic bags and waved it like a flag. "I give credit where credit is due—Han Ting."

She grabbed the take-out container with the rice and dug a spoon into it. "I'm impressed that you followed me into the forest, without my knowledge, and then ran toward me when you heard me scream. Rice?"

"Please." He shoved both plates toward her and opened another container.

They piled their plates high with food, Finn poured the wine she brought into the two waiting glasses, and they sat down across from each other. "This is a nice place, remote but not too far from civilization. At least you have a few neighbors on the water."

"Blood money." He tore into a packet of soy sauce and dumped it over his food. "Settlement from my dad's accident."

"I'm sure he would've approved of this place, close to nature and the things you love." She plucked a piece of chicken from her plate and pointed at Bodhi. Finn nodded.

"I think he would've been happier had I stayed with law enforcement. That was his dream job for me."

"Yeah, well, parents aren't supposed to have dream jobs for their kids." She broke apart a pair of chopsticks and clicked them together. "But at least your dad had dreams for you. My mom's dreams included the government money she got for two kids. She would've been even happier to collect for a third, my half brother, but he was a few years younger than I and someone in the neighborhood tattled on her, so protective services whisked him away."

"Have you ever tried to track him down?"

"It was a closed adoption." She shrugged, trying to make light of the pain she felt when children's services snatched away her baby brother. "Tiffany had made some strides in locating him, but she never had a chance to share any of that with me. I started from scratch recently. I even hired some-one to help. She's made a few inquiries, but no luck so far."

"Have you been back to the house where you grew up? I remember it wasn't far from here. On the other side of the peninsula by Bangor Base, right?"

"That's right. I took you there once. It was the only sta-bility in Mom's life. A navy buddy of my grandfather's owned the place and let us live there for cheap. Wasn't much of a house." She gave an exaggerated shiver, shim-mying her shoulders. "I wouldn't go back there now. Noth-ing but bad memories."

"I'm sorry. That must've been a tough life for you girls. If Tiffany protected you in that environment, I understand why it's so important for you to get justice for her."

"She *did* protect me, but it was at her expense. She fig-ured as long as she could keep the attention of Mom's sleazy boyfriends on her and away from me, she was doing her job as a big sister. I mean, it only makes sense she would turn to drugs and sex work after a childhood like that." Jessica's eyes watered and she sniffed, but it wasn't due to the spicy beef she'd just popped into her mouth.

"It makes sense. Tiffany was a hero. Hey—" he aimed a chopstick at her "—I discovered something interesting today, or rather some*one* interesting. Did Tiffany ever men-tion a guy named Deke Macy to you?"

"Deke Macy. Doesn't sound familiar. Who is he?"

He explained to her how he'd checked out the greeting cards in the student store and landed in Deke Macy's office.

Finn said, "He had a creepy attitude toward the young women on campus."

"Sounds like a loser, but what would he have to do with Tiffany?"

"I found out from the accounting supervisor in the office, Nia, that Deke has been working at the university for about twelve years, and he started in food service…like Tiffany."

"Oh my God, yeah. If he was still working food service ten years ago, he would've worked with my sister. Did he mention Tiffany?"

"No, that's the weird thing. We were discussing the current campus murders, so you'd think he would've brought up the fact that he'd worked with a previous murder victim."

"Maybe, but why be so obvious about his attraction to the young women on campus? He had to know that would be a red flag for you, or anyone. You didn't hear him laugh, did you? There would be no mistaking that laugh."

"Nope." Finn maneuvered a piece of chicken with his chopsticks. "He must already have a reputation on campus. Why try to pretend or hide it now? The kids seem to call him Dick instead of Deke."

Jessica started to smirk and then stopped. "Wait. Dick does sound familiar. Tiffany used to talk a lot about her coworkers because it was her first real job, and I remember her joking about some guy named Dick. What are you going to do with this information?"

"Already done. I reported my conversation with Deke to Detective Morse. I mean, there's more. Both Morgan and Missy worked on campus in the university bookstore complex. The student employees who open and close the registers have to pick up and drop off the cash at accounting. Deke's office is in the accounting area."

"So Morgan and Missy were in that office, near Deke?"

"That, I don't know. Nia, the accounting manager, doesn't remember either of the girls being regulars." He took a sip of wine. "Doesn't mean they weren't there, and Deke didn't know them. What did you discover today?"

She jabbed a finger at him. "You uncovered a person of interest. I just remembered my sister's favorite color."

"What's the significance of your sister's favorite color?" He wiped his mouth with a paper towel and crumpled it in his hand. "I have those files you asked for, by the way. I pulled them out of my garage when I got home."

"Red. We found red fibers on Missy, just like at Morgan's crime scene. Missy had them under her fingernails, and I discovered more in the area. Tiffany's favorite color was red. The sympathy card references red. Maybe there's some significance there. Neither of the women was wearing anything red, so it didn't come from them."

Finn said, "It's a reach."

At least he hadn't rolled his eyes. "I know that, but I'm looking at everything through the lens of Tiffany's case. For whatever reason, whether this guy murdered Tiffany or not, he's got a thing for her homicide. He duplicated it with these two victims—same manner of death, same location, and he's involving me in his crime spree."

He aimed his chopsticks at the kitchen counter behind her. "More food? I forgot I bought egg rolls, too."

"No, I'm good." She stretched and finished her glass of wine. "I'll clean up in here while you bring in the box. We can look at it on this table?"

"That works."

Finn pushed back from the table, and she collected the dishes, rinsed them and put them in the dishwasher. Jessica closed up the boxes of leftover food and stacked them in the fridge, which seemed fairly well stocked for a bachelor.

Bodhi kept her company, hoping for a stray morsel of

food, and she obliged with several. As she held the paper bag, greasy with the eggrolls inside, Finn walked past her and snatched the bag from her hand.

"I'm gonna need at least one of these with my second glass of wine. I can't drink the stuff without food." He dumped the egg rolls onto a plate and popped the lids on the sweet-and-sour sauce and spicy mustard. He then grabbed the bottle of wine from the fridge and returned to the table to fill their glasses.

Her pulse jumped when she saw the cardboard box on the floor next to the table. Wiping her hands on a dish towel, she said, "I'm ready."

As he sat next to her at the table and kicked the lid off the box, he said, "I have...crime scene photos in here. I can separate them, if you like."

"I've seen them before, but you can leave them in the box as long as there's a list of Tiffany's clothing." She took a gulp of wine.

"There is. I'll have a look at the people the detectives questioned, too. Maybe Deke's one of them." He bent over, shuffling through the files in the box. He dropped a couple of folders on the table, and little puffs of dust made her sneeze.

"Sorry about that." He hopped up from his seat and grabbed a few paper towels from the kitchen. When he sat down, he wiped down both folders, front and back.

He shoved one toward her with his finger. "You should be able to find her clothing in there."

Her hand trembled slightly when she reached for the file. Holding her breath, she flipped it open. Words, just words. Neatly typed words on a page to summarize a whole life.

She skimmed the first few pages until she came to a description of the body at the scene. She skipped the gruesome details, which she could recite by heart anyway, and zeroed in on the items her sister was wearing. Pictures of the clothing followed.

Jessica smiled at the skinny jeans with embroidery on the pocket. Tiffany loved those jeans. She'd paired them with a white midriff top, which superthin Tiffany could carry off, and a denim trucker jacket with more embroidery on the back—none of it in red. She finished off the outfit with a pair of white wedge sneakers.

Jessica slumped in her chair and took another slug of wine. "Nothing red. No red fibers found on her body, either. Did Deke's name come up?"

Finn held up a piece of paper with names printed out in different groups. He shook it in the air. "He's listed under coworkers."

"Wow, so he *did* know Tiffany. This is significant. Any notes on his interview?"

"Looking at this, it doesn't seem as if her coworkers were grilled. Probably someone talked to them in a group— Tiffany complain about anyone, anyone hanging around her—those kinds of questions. Unless one of them had something interesting to add, they probably weren't questioned further."

"If Deke killed her, he wouldn't have been drawing attention to himself. It could be him, Finn."

"When I called Detective Morse this afternoon, I did mention that Deke may have worked with Tiffany back when she was murdered. He's a good detective. He'll discover this. My guess is that Deke has an interview with the sheriff's department in his future."

"You should've never given up police work." She pinched

an egg roll between her fingers and dipped it in the red sauce.

"Wasn't for me. You know better than anyone, I couldn't follow the rules." He swirled his wine in his glass. "After all, I broke them for you."

"I don't think you're the kind of person who would do something unless you wanted to do it. I didn't think it then; I don't think it now." She crunched into her egg roll with her teeth.

"Oh, I wanted to do it. I wanted to do it for you. There was probably nothing I wouldn't have done for you...at the time."

She dabbed her mouth. "And now?"

"I think it's clear nothing's changed."

She should've never eaten that greasy egg roll. She wiped her hands with a paper towel, swished a sip of wine in her mouth and stood up, all while keeping contact with Finn's blue eyes.

She skirted the table, placed her hands on his shoulders, leaned over and kissed him. His mouth opened, and his soft lips caressed hers, gentle at first and then pressing with an urgency akin to her own.

She murmured against his lips, "That's more like it."

He acted on her encouragement, slipping a hand into the strands of her hair, cupping the back of her head and drawing her in closer. This time his kiss scorched her lips, branding her somewhere deep inside, taking possession of her soul. If she'd had any doubts before that the boy had grown into a man, this kiss torched those doubts and turned them to ash.

He pulled her into his lap, and she straddled him, the tip of her shoe resting against the box that contained her sister's case files. As she toyed with the edge of his T-shirt, she asked, "Do you have a bedroom in this hideaway?"

Without missing a beat, Finn stood up with her legs wrapped around his waist. Bodhi thumped his tail a couple of times as Finn stepped over him on the way to the bedroom.

Finn nudged the door open with his foot and turned slowly in the middle of the room, so she could get the full effect of the large wall of glass facing the dark ripples of the bay.

As he placed her on the bed, she huffed out a breath, curling her legs beneath her. "Anyone could be out there in a boat, peering into your house."

He reached across her and fumbled with a remote. A set of dark drapes automatically slid across the window, casting the room in blackness. He tapped on a small bedside lamp. "Is that better?"

"I'll tell you in a minute." She gathered handfuls of his shirt and tugged.

He raised his arms, and she sat up on her knees to pull the shirt over his head. Running her hands along the hard ridge of muscle on his chest, she planted a kiss on his collarbone. "How does a professor get this hard?"

"I'll tell you in a minute."

Giggling like a tipsy sorority girl, Jessica fell back on the bed and pulled her phone from the pocket of her sweater. She placed it on the nightstand, next to the light highlighting all the bulges and planes of Finn's half-naked torso.

She shrugged out of the sweater. "I need to catch up."

"I can help you with that." Placing his knees on either side of her hips, he peeled her shirt from her body and yanked it over her head. He tossed it over his shoulder as she scrambled out of her bra.

He caught his breath and whispered, "Beautiful."

She arched her back, and he fitted one hand against her spine while he pressed a trail of kisses from her throat to her belly. She squirmed beneath him, heat searing through her veins.

Hooking his finger in the waistband of her jeans, he said, "You're gonna have to stop wriggling around like that. I'm only human."

"Prove it." Her fingers clawed at the button on his fly, but her impatient hands couldn't do the deed.

He unzipped and yanked his jeans and briefs down his muscled thighs. He rolled off the bed to kick them off, and she took the opportunity to shimmy out of her own jeans and the socks still covering her feet.

Bodhi's soft head brushed her foot as he absconded with one of her socks, but the dog was in luck tonight as she had other things on her mind.

When Finn joined her on the bed, he stretched out beside her, and their busy hands explored each other's bodies. They punctuated their exploration with hungry kisses, prolonging the buildup to excruciating heights.

She waited ten years for this; what was five or ten minutes until ecstasy?

Her cell phone buzzed on the nightstand. She laced her fingers through Finn's hair as he imprinted a row of kisses down the inside of her thigh.

"I have to see who it is, in case it's my boss."

Finn growled in the back of his throat, but he rolled to his side as she scooted up and reached over to slide her phone from the nightstand.

Finn's rough voice came from somewhere near her left hip. "Is it your boss?"

She stared at the name and bit the inside of her cheek. "It's Ashley King. It might be important."

Finn grumbled. "It's after ten."

"That's why it might be important." She tapped the incoming call. "What's wrong, Ashley?"

"Sorry to bother you, sweetie, but you wanted me to tell you if I remembered anything else about the time Tiff died."

"I did." Jessica's heart, which had just started to slow down from Finn's attentions, ramped up again and she put her phone on speaker, so Finn could hear. "What did you remember?"

Ashley coughed her smoker's cough. "Something else was stolen from the apartment with that damned doll."

"What was it?" She glanced at Finn, a stack of pillows propping up his head, his gaze sharp.

"Her knitting."

"Knitting? Tiffany didn't knit."

"Crazy, I know, but she was trying to give up smoking and decided to learn how to knit. She was working on something—something for you at the time, and I swear it was taken with the doll because when you came over to collect her stuff, I asked you about it."

"I don't remember that at all."

"You were kinda messed up, sweetie. You hadn't found any knitting needles, so I figured they were taken like the doll. She worked on that damned red scarf every night."

Jessica's fingers curled into the bedspread beneath her. "Tiffany was knitting a red scarf at the time she was murdered?"

"That's right. You can ask Denny. Click, click, click those damned needles. She was working on that red scarf for you…and somebody stole it."

Chapter Eleven

"Sweetie?" Ashley's raspy voice grated across the line, but Jessica seemed incapable of speech, her round eyes glassy in the dim light.

"Ashley, this is Finn Karlsson, a…friend of Jessica's. You might remember me…"

"Oh, I remember you. Found our Tiff's body."

"That's right. I'm helping Jessica." He dragged a blanket up the bed and covered Jessica's shivering body with it. "This scarf Tiffany was knitting, how long was it? I mean how far along was she?"

"Far." She hacked again. "I'm not saying it was any good, but she was almost done with it. She knitted away with that thing curled up at her feet like some kind of red snake ready to strike. I told her one time, Jessie's tall, but hell, that thing could wrap around bigfoot's neck a few times."

Finn winced and squeezed Jessica's thigh beneath the blanket. "You never reported this theft to the police?"

"Like I told Jessie, I didn't think much about it—a doll and a beginner's knitting project. Didn't see the point. Didn't even make a connection with Tiff's murder, but I remembered it tonight when Denny and I were talking about Tiff, you know, good times, and we were joking about her knitting." Ashley sucked in a breath. "Jessie? Is Jessie okay?"

"I-I'm fine, Ashley." Jessica pulled the blanket more tightly around her form. "I really appreciate your call. Anything else you remember, please call me anytime."

"Okay. Didn't mean to interrupt you and Finn. I know you always had a crush on that cop, but at least he's not the po-po anymore."

Finn rolled his eyes at Jessica. "Yeah, thanks for that, Ashley."

Ashley ended the call after more assurances from Jessica that she was okay, even though neither one of them told Ashley the reason for Jessica's shock.

Jessica sat, hunched over, the phone in her lap. "Something old, something dead, something stolen, something red. It's the scarf, isn't it? He stole that scarf from Tiffany at the same time he stole the rag doll, and he's using it to strangle women."

Did he have an answer for her? Did he disagree with her, as fantastic as it all sounded? "But he didn't use that scarf to strangle Tiffany. The investigators are certain Plank—" Jessica shot him a look from beneath her lashes and he held up his hands "—or whoever killed your sister used a tie."

"That's right, even though Plank always used his hands, those big hands." She pulled the blanket up to her chin and pinned it to her chest. "The person who killed Morgan and Missy knows too much about Tiffany—things nobody else would know—not to have been involved in her homicide. That sick poem says it all. Tiffany's murder is old, she's dead, he stole a red scarf from her. It's all there, Finn."

"It's not all there. We have one person of interest. The cops can talk to Deke, and I'm sure they will after the info

I gave them about him, but you of all people know they'll have to find evidence. And why now?" Finn scooped up his jeans and untangled his briefs. "Why did he start up again if he's been living here all this time with access to plenty of young women?"

She pulled a pillow over her face and screamed into it.

That's exactly how he felt right now. Would he ever be able to date this woman without a murder getting in the way?

Peeking over the edge of the pillow, she said, "I'm sorry I took the call."

"No, you're not. We just got another vital piece of information that'll make Detective Morse take that poem in the sympathy card more seriously." He pulled on his jeans as he rose from the bed. "After hearing the phone ring, I doubt you would've been able to concentrate on the business at hand, anyway."

"I wouldn't be so sure about that." She quirked her eyebrows up and down.

"Let's call it a night. I need to let Bodhi outside."

At the sound of his name, Bodhi trotted into the room, a fuzzy black sock hanging from his jaws.

Finn pointed at his pet. "I think Bodhi got your sock. It'll never be the same again."

"He can keep it as a souvenir of the night his dad almost got laid."

"And what does his dad get as a memento?"

"You can have my other sock."

He tried to get her to spend the night at his place, as difficult as that would've been for him to have her sleeping in the next room. They both knew the mood had turned and although he would've given it the old college try, he knew Tiffany's murder consumed Jessica's thoughts, and he didn't want to compete. Tiffany's ghost already hovered over their relationship. He didn't want her haunting the first time he made love to Jessica.

But she insisted on spending the night at her own place, so Finn followed her outside and checked her car before allowing her to leave with promises she'd text him as soon as she got home and locked the doors.

This killer seemed more interested in taunting and tormenting Jessica than killing her, but you couldn't trust a psychopath. He was moving closer and closer to Jessica. He must have some sort of end game…and that end game just might be Jessica's death.

About thirty minutes later, as he finished up the egg rolls, sharing one with Bodhi, Jessica texted him. She thanked him for dinner, for the files, for the info on Deke, and for listening, couching all those words in a bunch of emojis. But nowhere in the text did she thank him for rocking her world.

Did that mean she regretted it?

Bodhi jumped on the couch next to him with Jessica's sock clenched between his teeth. Finn rubbed the dog's head. "I know you're happy with the spoils of the evening, but I wanted more…so much more."

THE FOLLOWING DAY, Jessica met with Deputy Alvarado regarding the physical evidence for Missy's homicide case. The evidence from Morgan's had already been packaged and shipped to the lab for additional testing, including DNA and possible latent fingerprints.

She'd be packaging the physical evidence from Missy's case and delivering it herself via the sheriff's van. The biological evidence from Missy's autopsy had already been sent to Seattle, including the red fibers, as it had been found beneath Missy's fingernails. Had she tried to remove the red scarf tightening around her throat? Did the killer have this in his hands when he was leading her down the trail to Missy?

She spoke to Alvarado without lifting her head. "Did you see the red fibers before they were sent to Seattle for DNA testing? It could be yarn, couldn't it?"

"Could be." Alvarado smacked the table. "That Deke Macy is bald, shaved head. Might explain why there's no hair left at the scene. Or maybe the killer wore a beanie, tucking his hair in, and this is a fiber from that."

"Or it's the murder weapon. He used it for Morgan, too." She dropped another plastic bag into the pouch. "Have you heard anything more about Macy?"

"I know Detective Morse brought him in for questioning. He may have worked with both murdered women, or at least had contact with them."

Jessica murmured, "And he worked with my sister, Tiffany Hunt, at the time of her murder ten years ago."

Alvarado put down his clipboard where he'd been checking off the items as she put them in the pouch. "I heard about that, Jessica. I'm so sorry. I had a sister who was murdered by her ex-boyfriend—domestic violence case. I know it's tough."

Her gaze flew to his face. "I'm so sorry."

"It's hard to fathom a guy like Macy getting away with one murder and holding off for ten years before committing his next."

"That's true, but maybe he committed crimes while he was on vacation or visiting someone." She dropped the last item into the pouch as Alvarado marked it off on his form.

"I'm just hoping he's our guy and no other young women are in danger."

"I hope so, too. Detective Morse will get to the truth." He scrawled his signature on the form and held it out for her to sign.

They didn't get to the truth of Tiffany's murder.

Jessica added her signature and tucked the form into the pouch. She had already placed the rag doll and the sympathy card in separate bags to bring to the lab, but the sheriff's department wouldn't allow them to be labeled with the official evidence, as she'd already destroyed the chain of custody several times over.

"I'll be phoning in for updates. Can I contact you, Deputy Alvarado?"

"Call me Tomas, and you can." He jerked his thumb at the door. "Wait in the lobby of the station. Deputy Davis is driving the van over."

"Thanks." She slung the pouch over her shoulder and headed for the lobby. She peeked down the corridor, wondering if Morse was grilling Macy behind one of those doors.

After Finn had told her about Deke Macy, she'd looked him up online. Didn't have much of a social media presence. Mostly followed young Instagram models, liking their sexy poses and posting emojis with tongues hanging out. Finn had been right. If he was trying to hide his dirty deeds, he was hiding in plain sight. Of course, that could be a ruse, too—the *do you think I'm that stupid* defense.

Avery Plank had lurked beneath the radar—not exactly a family man, had one divorce and one daughter in his past—but he'd been a respected engineer in his field. He'd escaped his rough childhood, as she had, but the darkness had seeped too far into his soul for him to evade it.

"Ms. Eller?"

She jumped and spun around to come face-to-face with a beefy deputy who looked like he could be a defensive lineman for the Seattle Seahawks. She'd be safe with him.

"Deputy Davis? You can call me Jessica."

"And you can call me Kimani, CSI lady." He patted the pouch. "I'll need to check the form before we get in the van."

She hoisted the bag onto a table in the lobby and slipped out the form. She placed it on the table next to the bag.

He scanned the form and glanced in the bag. "You have two other paper bags coming with us?"

"In my car, not official evidence."

"I'll follow you."

He followed her to her car where she retrieved the two paper bags, and then they got settled in the van for the ninety-minute ride to Marysville, including the ferry across the Sound.

As Jessica adjusted her seat belt, she asked, "You ever play football?"

"Why, yes, ma'am. Washington State Cougars. How could you tell?"

"Ah, because you're as broad as a double-wide trailer, and I mean that in the most complimentary way."

He chuckled. "My wife would take exception. She keeps telling me I don't need to eat like I'm still making those tackles."

She and Kimani chatted easily about football, the King County Sheriff's Department, living on the Sound and his wife's cooking, anything to keep her mind off what was happening to Deke Macy back at the station. Had she ever seen the guy before? If he was the killer, he must know who she was. Knew her car. Had followed her. Had her phone number. The knowledge made her feel slightly nauseous, and she cracked the window.

The hour-and-a-half ride went by fast, and they'd missed most of the traffic, but by the time Kimani pulled the van into the parking lot of the forensic lab, Jessica was ready to stretch her legs.

Kimani parked outside the vehicle inspection center where a few cars perched on hydraulic lifts, ready for a thorough search. She knew several people in that unit, and they'd pull plants from the undercarriage and dig out seeds from the tires in an effort to glean every bit of evidence they could from a suspect's or victim's car. Too bad neither of the crimes on campus involved vehicles.

She hopped from the van and Kimani grabbed the pouch from the back. As he handed it to her, he said, "I'm escorting you to Evidence Receiving, and then I'm going to get some lunch and head back. Are you coming with me or staying?"

"I'll be staying for a while. I can probably hijack one of our vans to go back to Kitsap."

They parted ways at Evidence Receiving when Jessica handed the pouch over to Nicole Meloan, the supervisor. She shook the paper bags at her. "A couple of things in here I'd like tested, but I compromised the chain of evidence because I found them on my own, and in the case of the doll, I carried it around with me."

Nicole clicked her tongue. "Michael know about your little faux pas?"

"I told him. He was…disappointed."

"This evidence won't be in lockup long. I've had lab rats knocking on my door all morning looking for it."

"There's not much to paw over, and the evidence that might contain DNA has been sent to Seattle."

Nicole unzipped the pouch and plucked out the form. "I hear that's on a rush, too."

"Have you heard anything else? The sheriff's department is questioning a person of interest. He may have worked with both women...and he was there ten years ago when my sister was murdered."

Nicole put a gloved hand on her arm. "Do you think these cases are linked to Tiffany's?"

Flicking her finger at the paper bags on the table, Jessica answered. "That's what these are all about—a card that mentions my sister's name and a doll that may be one my sister had in her possession at the time of her murder."

"You're kidding. That's significant...and scary for you. Are you all right?" Nicole's dark brown eyes got huge. "Wait, is that why you found the second victim? This guy told you where she was?"

Jessica told her the story of the text, the meeting that never happened and how the killer lured her to Missy's body. "It was awful. Somehow discovering a body like that was a hundred times worse than coming into a murder scene where dozens of cops and CSIs are already roaming around."

"I can imagine." Nicole waved her arms around the room, shelves stacked with boxes, plastic and paper bags. "It's all so sterile in here. Anyway, I haven't heard anything about a person of interest yet."

"I'm keeping my fingers crossed." Jessica tapped the form on the table. "Initial this, so I can get out of here and go find Michael."

Jessica passed by several of the labs where the techs

would soon be analyzing the evidence from Missy's homicide. She made a right turn at the end of the hallway and tapped on Michael's open door.

He glanced up and waved her in, rolling his eyes and pointing at the phone. He'd just dashed her hopes that he'd be in a good mood and this interview would go better than she deserved.

When he ended the call, he dropped the phone on his desk and dragged his hands through his black hair, which made his light blue eyes even more startling when he skewered her with his gaze.

"So, Nancy Drew is back in the lab."

"Yeah, so funny." She plopped in one of the two chairs facing his desk without an invitation. "But Nancy's the one who found Missy Park minutes after her death. The cops could've caught the guy right then and there."

"He must've had some sort of escape plan mapped out in advance, knowing you'd find the body and report it right away." Her boss steepled his long fingers. "I heard Finn Karlsson was on the scene with you."

"He was there. We've been in touch since I've been in Kitsap."

"He's writing a book about Plank. Did he tell you that?"

"Y-yes." Eventually. "But he's going to have to write an addendum when we find out Plank didn't murder my sister."

"Deke Macy is not looking like the guy for these crimes, though."

"Really?" Her head jerked up. "Who says?"

"King County Sheriff's Department. Just got off the phone with one of the deputies. Macy has an alibi for both murders. Have to be checked out, of course, but easy to find out if he's lying." He held up his hands. "Suspects lie about alibis all the time, knowing full well the investigators can figure that out after a few phone calls, interviews or camera footage. Could still be the guy."

"But unlikely." Jessica slumped in her seat. "I knew he was too good to be true. Creepy dude icking on college coeds and following young Instagram models—and not trying to hide it."

Michael narrowed his icy eyes. "Sounds like you did quite a bit of your own research on the creepy Mr. Macy."

"He worked with Tiffany ten years ago."

"If you want to be a cop, Jessica, go to the academy and be one. If you want to be a top-notch forensics investigator, do your job."

"Like you didn't do your own investigating once upon a time."

"Yeah, that was because I was accused of murder."

His office phone rang, and he dropped his gaze to the display. "Sheriff's department again. Maybe Deke Macy did lie. Wilder here."

Jessica studied Michael's impassive face, which gave away nothing.

"I see. Good. Rush job. Yeah." When he ended the call, Jessica was none the wiser.

"Did he lie about his alibis?"

"No, but something almost as encouraging. They found trace DNA on both sets of red fibers…and it doesn't match the victims' DNA reference samples."

Chapter Twelve

"How did they get those results so quickly?" Finn pushed a piece of crinkly yellow wax paper piled with french fries toward Jessica, sitting in his office visitor chair. She'd driven straight to campus from the forensics lab in Marysville once she'd discovered he was working late.

"The lab got the victims' DNA, called a reference sample, right away so they can rule them out when they start processing the evidence. Further tests can then be done if the samples show similarities. They discovered the trace DNA on the red fibers from Morgan's crime scene right away and started processing that. They're still testing and analyzing it to see if there's enough to send through CODIS." She pinched a french fry from his offering and bit off the end. "Did you know that Morgan's family owns the biggest logging enterprise in the state?"

"I thought I heard something like that. Are you telling me Morgan is getting special treatment because of her family?" He clapped a hand over his mouth. "I'm shocked. Just shocked."

"I mean, I'm glad she is, but every victim deserves special treatment and fast-tracked results. Avery Plank's sex worker victims sure didn't get any such consideration. The DNA on those cases took weeks, even months."

"At least Missy benefits from the Flemmings' connections." Finn dusted the salt from his fingers onto the paper bag that had contained his dinner. "Deke Macy is a disappointing suspect. His two alibis look solid—at a karaoke bar one night where several patrons have already attested to his horrible singing and down in Seattle visiting his brother on the other night."

"Family members lie all the time. Hell, his brother could even be involved." She wedged a shoe on the edge of his desk. "Why are you working so late in your office? You can't grade those exams on your laptop at home?"

"I'm giving another exam on Monday, and I promised my students extended office hours. I started grading, got hungry, ordered food and by the time the students' visits trailed off, I was on a roll. Told myself I'd finish here."

"And I interrupted you."

"I was almost done, and I wanted to hear about the DNA tests. You said the lab hasn't run the DNA through CODIS yet."

"Not yet. They had the victims' reference samples, so they were able to test it against those, and there's no match to the victims' samples." She rubbed her hands together. "Let's hope they get enough of the sample to run through CODIS, and that there's a match."

He offered her the rest of the fries, and she declined, so he scrunched up the paper and shoved it into the plastic bag. "There was never any DNA recovered at your sister's crime scene, so it's not going to help there."

"No, but I'm certain there will be a connection. I could've gone along with the theory that someone was playing stupid games with my tires and even the doll, but that speculation ended when he led me to Missy's body. The person leaving me clues is the same person who murdered Morgan and Missy."

"You're right, but it doesn't necessarily mean he killed Tiffany. Could be a copycat." Finn pushed back from his desk and grabbed the plastic bag by the handle. "I'm going to drop this in the trash can in the hallway, so the smell doesn't linger in my office."

He squeezed past her chair and pushed open the door, which he'd left ajar. As he stepped out of his office, a shadow flashed at the end of the darkened corridor. He called out. "Hello? It's Professor Karlsson. Did you need to see me?"

A flurry of footsteps echoed from around the corner, and Finn's cop instincts spurred him on to give chase. "Hey!"

He took off running down the smooth hallway in his loafers, slipping every few feet until he reached the end of the corridor. Finn skidded around the corner, and the side door at the bottom of the stairs slammed shut.

He loped downstairs, hanging on to the banister, taking two steps at a time. When he hit the bottom, he scrambled for the door and heaved his body against it to shove it open, stumbling into the small quad.

Panting, Finn stopped and scanned the trees that bordered the quad, his gaze darting back and forth between the two walkways—one leading into the main quad in the front of the building and the other skirting another lecture hall.

He crept silently to the corner of the building and peered around the edge. When the door burst open behind him, he spun around.

Jessica careened around the corner and almost bumped into him standing still in the front quad. She drew herself up and grabbed his sleeve. "What's going on? Why did you take off like that?"

"There was someone lurking in the hallway outside my office. I thought it might be a student thinking I was busy, but when I called to him, he took off."

"Him? Are you sure it was a man?"

"Yeah. I just saw his shadow, but he moved like a guy." Finn wiped the back of his hand across his brow. "Why would he take off like that?"

"Is there anything to steal up there? Any reason to be there other than to see a professor?"

"Shouldn't be anything to steal. All the offices are locked up. There are classrooms on the first floor, but the second floor is the humanities office and the professors' officers. The humanities office is locked, too."

"Were there any other professors holding office hours?" She glanced up at the building sporting a few lights in the windows. "Maybe he was there to see someone else."

"Professor Godwin was working late, but he left about thirty minutes before you arrived." He pushed his hair back from his forehead, his adrenaline rush seeping from his system. "Why would any student of Godwin's take off running from another professor in the building? The doors are locked, but it's not like students aren't allowed in the halls. They are. You can even go into a lecture hall after hours and sit down if you want. The university holds some night classes, some extension classes."

Jessica settled her back against the rough stone of the building and crossed her arms. "What do you think he was doing there, and why do you think he ran?"

"Did you notice anyone following you here when you got to town?"

She licked her lips and her gaze flickered over his shoulder to the empty quad. "I drove here straight from the forensics lab. Someone would've had to have been following me for a long time."

"I think the person was trying to spy on us. Listen to our conversation. I never completely close my office door unless I'm alone. I'd left it ajar, and anyone in the corridor could've heard our conversation. Voices carry down that hall, so the person wouldn't have even had to have been that close. He heard me announce that I was going to throw the trash into the can and started moving toward the stairs."

"Why would someone be spying on us?"

"I don't know. We've been asking a lot of questions of a lot of people. I questioned Macy and the cops knock on his door the next day. He must know I put them onto him."

She rubbed her arms. "Do you think that was Deke?"

"Wish I had caught up with this guy." He glanced at his useless shoes. "Should've worn some running shoes to class."

"I think I left your door wide open when I followed you out here." She pushed off the wall. "Maybe he came back and stole something."

"To do that, he would've had to run out here to the main quad, and then circle back into the building from the front. I think he was more concerned with getting away. He couldn't have known you'd follow me, anyway."

"Unless he was hoping to find me alone in your office."

Grabbing her hand, he tugged her. "Let's take a look."

He led her to the main entrance to Waverly Hall, one of the four lecture halls that fronted the quad. Head down, he studied the steps to the front door. "If he came this way, he would've left footprints from the wet grass we went through to get here. I don't see anything, do you?"

Jessica lifted her own foot, leaving a damp imprint on

the step. "None but ours, but his could've dried by now. We stepped in some dewy grass, not the Sound."

One of the double doors to Waverly stood open and yellow light spilled onto the steps. Finn asked, "Is this how you came into the building earlier?"

"It's the only way I knew how before you went charging out of that side door. Didn't see anyone, and nobody followed me." She ascended the remaining steps and stepped into the building. "Maybe someone was after you this time."

THE FOLLOWING EVENING, Jessica got ready for the university's candlelight vigil in honor of both Morgan and Missy. The gathering had several functions—to pay respect to the women, of course, but also as an informational safety meeting for the students and although not advertised, law enforcement would use it to scan the crowd for unusual activity or people.

Jessica knew she'd be keeping a sharp eye out for the latter. The spy at Waverly Hall last night had scared her more than she'd let on to Finn. If the person had been an innocent student, why not stop when Finn spotted him?

Would the killer really be so bold as to try to eavesdrop in an empty college building? What would've happened if Finn had caught this person? The killer didn't use a knife or gun on his victims, but that didn't mean he didn't carry a weapon. She knew Finn had a conceal-carry permit from his days as a cop, but the university didn't allow guns on campus—and that rule extended to the professors.

She tucked her own weapon in her purse. It might extend to visitors, too, but she was a member of the Washington State Patrol. She could make a strong case for carrying.

Finn had come to campus today for a department meeting and had stayed in his office marking papers and entering midterm grades. Was he hoping to catch the spy again? She planned to meet him at his office and attend the vigil with him. It wouldn't take them long to get there as the main quad right outside his building was hosting the gathering.

She grabbed a jacket on her way out of the hotel room and waved to the clerk as she stepped outside. She texted Finn before starting the drive to the university. She didn't want him thinking she was the spy creeping up on his office.

When she reached the campus, traffic came to a stop. The regular lots were already full, a couple of TV news vans taking up more than their share of spaces.

Jessica turned onto the side street where she usually parked and took the back way to the campus. She used the newly discovered side door to Waverly Hall and tripped up the steps, making sure her low-heeled boots made plenty of noise.

She nodded to another professor heading down the hallway on her way to Finn's office. His door stood wide open, but she tapped anyway as he hunched over his laptop completely absorbed.

"Hey, Professor Karlsson, what can I do to get an A on my test." She batted her lashes when he glanced up. "I'll do *anything.*"

He rubbed his eyes with the heels of his hands. "Damn, I thought that was a legitimate offer coming my way."

She made a face at him. "You've been hanging around Deke Macy too long. His ick is rubbing off on you."

"Speaking of old Deke. I heard from my buddy at the sheriff's department, and that karaoke alibi for Morgan's murder is rock solid. They found security cam footage of him at the bar well before and after her time of death."

"I thought it might be too good to be true." She wedged a shoulder against his doorjamb. "Are you ready? It's getting crowded out there."

"I got halfway through the grading." He closed his laptop and packed up his bag. "I'm going to keep my stuff here. I don't want to take it down with me, and I don't want to leave it in the car."

"The campus police are out in force tonight. I'm sure Detective Morse is going to be looking at all the male attendees very closely."

"I know he's going to have a few deputies in plain clothes, too." Finn stood up and stretched, and Jessica wondered, not for the first time, how all his female students managed to concentrate in class.

He swiveled around to a filing cabinet and swung back, holding out two small votive candles in jars. "One for you. Someone from the Women Against Violence Against Women came through the offices today handing these out for the vigil."

"Someone will have lighters down there?"

"I'm sure of it." He emerged from behind the desk and lifted his jacket from the hook on the back of the door. "Let's do this."

When they exited the front of Waverly Hall, they joined a surge of people carrying candles and signs. Some of the girls were already crying. Jessica gritted her teeth, preparing for a rough night.

People were walking around with lighters and Jessica and Finn held out their candles to join the sea of lights bobbing on the quad. The sheriff's department took the stage first, and Detective Morse's distinct red hair blazed from the center of the group.

As she and Finn staked out a place at the edge of the crowd, a deputy approached Finn.

"Professor Karlsson, can we please have you join us on stage again? You don't have to speak this time, but you're a popular professor and the students will feel comfortable seeing you up there with all us cops."

Finn opened his mouth and turned to Jessica, but she nudged him. "Go ahead. You'll probably have a better view of all the attendees up there. If I spot someone suspicious, I'll text you."

"Meet me back at my office when this is all over."

She watched Finn's back as he and the deputy made their way to the stage. Then she cupped the candle in her hand and scanned the crowd. Even without high heels, Jessica's height allowed her to see over a lot of heads—not that there was much to see. Many people wore hoodies, the ovals of their faces dimly illuminated by the candles in their hands.

When Detective Morse tapped the microphone, Jessica swiveled her attention to the stage. Finn stood behind Morse along with several other people—both civilian and law enforcement. An Asian couple stood to the side of Morse. Their faces, masks of shock and grief, flagged them as Missy's parents.

Jessica studied the other expressions and found another couple with the same hollowed-out look on their faces. She recognized Matt Flemming from the online articles she'd looked up, but his appearance tonight bore little resemblance to the confident and powerful businessman who smiled in his pictures. Position and money might help speed up an investigation, but they could never bring back his little girl.

Jessica blinked back her own tears and tried to tune in to Morse's speech. He repeated much of what he said the other day about staying vigilant and keeping off the trails by the creek. He advised women to travel in groups and report any suspicious activity. Same stuff women had been hearing for years. When were the cops going to catch this guy?

Apparently, that thought had occurred to other women as well. A few disgruntled voices in the crowd yelled questions as if Morse were conducting a press conference. Shouts rang out asking for accountability. For suspects. Status on Deke Macy.

Jessica actually felt bad for the guy, whose face was turning the same color as his hair. She knew firsthand the deputies didn't have many leads. Their one good suspect had alibis. But the crowd wasn't having it.

People from the back surged forward, nudging Jessica into the person in front of her as someone stepped on her heel and apologized. This could get ugly.

Her cell phone buzzed in her pocket, and she pulled it out. Had Finn had enough? When she glanced at the display, her blood ran cold. An unknown number.

She tapped the text with her shaky thumb, and her breath hitched in her throat when she read the message. Getting rowdy

She didn't need to ask the sender's identity. Are you here?

I was. Took a break from the crowd with a friend

Her heart beat so hard, it rattled the buttons on her jacket. She texted him a flurry of questions. Where was he? Who was he with? Had he hurt anyone?

A throng of people rushed toward the stage, hoisting signs and screaming for answers. Someone bumped her elbow, knocking her phone to the ground. She dropped down to retrieve it, and then crawled away from the mob to the perimeter.

She blew out her candle and rolled onto the damp grass. On her knees, she held her phone close to her face, watching the bubbles on the display, waiting for his answers to her queries.

Art garden fountain maybe u won't be too late this time

Jessica staggered to her feet, jerking her head toward the stage. Finn, his head dipped, was in conversation with Morgan's father. Jessica waved her arms at him to get his attention, but more people and their signs got between her and her view of the stage.

She stabbed at Finn's phone number in her contacts. It rang three times and rolled over to voicemail. She shouted into the phone. "Come to the Art Garden."

She then grabbed the nearest person and yanked his arm. "Come to the Art Garden with me. There's another woman in danger."

The man shook her off and raised his fist at the stage. She tried getting the attention of another man, but if he could even hear her, he didn't seem interested in what she had to say.

As she started running along the side of Waverly Hall, she fumbled with her phone, forwarding the unknown caller's text to Finn. She wound up in the smaller quad where Finn had chased the spy. She headed for the walkway that led to the Art Garden, a garden filled with sculptures that fronted the fine arts building.

Panting, she thumbed 911 into her phone. "Send the police. I'm heading toward the Art Garden on campus. I have reason to believe someone is in danger."

"How do you know this, ma'am?"

"Somebody texted me a threat. The cops are already here on campus. Send a few to the Art Garden."

"Someone texted you?"

"Oh, for God's sake. I see someone in the Art Garden with a gun. Send the police."

Gripping her phone in one hand, Jessica pulled her weapon from her purse with the other. She hadn't been lying to the 911 operator. There was going to be someone in the Art Garden with a gun in a few seconds.

She made it to the path that wound its way through shrubbery and flower beds, a sculpture positioned every few feet. The fountain gurgled in the middle of all this beauty and art, and Jessica made a beeline toward it, holding her gun in front of her.

"Where are you? The police are on the way."

She rushed toward the fountain and almost tripped over a body on the ground at the edge. She cried out, "Not again. Not again."

As she collapsed next to the still form, her gun hanging at her side, someone barreled into her back, driving her over the edge of the fountain. A gloved hand gripped the back of her neck and shoved her head into the water.

She tried to roll to her side, twist her head, but her attacker had his weight against her hips and his hand in her hair, keeping her head submerged. She couldn't move... and she couldn't breathe.

Chapter Thirteen

As he bent his head toward Mr. Flemming, Finn felt his phone buzz in his pocket with a text message. When Mr. Flemming turned to his wife, Finn glanced up at the unruly mob. He understood the students' frustration, but this was not the time or place to vent those frustrations.

His gaze scanned the crowd, trying to pick out Jessica's blond hair. He caught sight of her on the edge of the pressing throng of people, moving away from the quad.

He patted his pocket and pulled out his phone. He had a missed phone call he hadn't even heard due to the shouts and chants. The text message was from Jessica, a forwarded text message.

He squinted at the display as if that could help him make sense of the cryptic message. Art Garden. Fountain. Too late.

Understanding slammed into his chest so hard, he gasped. He jerked his head up, zeroing in on where he'd last seen Jessica. She'd disappeared.

Adrenaline flooded his body and his limbs jerked. He touched Mr. Flemming's arm. "Excuse me."

Finn ducked back from the grouping on the stage and cranked his head back and forth, looking for a cop other than Detective Morse—who was trying to field questions from a horde of angry and agitated people. The majority of the deputies were among the crowd, some at the front of the stage to make sure the irate mourners didn't overrun it.

He'd have to go it alone. He jumped from the stage, grateful he'd swapped his loafers for a pair of running shoes. Maybe he'd had a feeling he'd need to run. So he did.

Finn took off, skirting the perimeter of the crowd, in the direction of the Art Garden. He dashed across the smaller quad behind Waverly Hall and took the walkway toward the art building, Callahan Hall.

As soon as he stepped foot in the Art Garden, he started calling Jessica's name. More than anything, he just wanted her to stop. To turn around and wait for him. Was he too late as the text message had taunted?

He broke onto the pebbled surface that surrounded the fountain and his stomach dropped when he spotted two bodies next to the fountain.

As he ran toward them, a figure appeared behind him, and he swung around, his fist bunched.

"Whoa." A deputy in uniform held up his hands. "Do you have the gun?"

Finn ignored his question. "There are two injured women here."

When Finn dropped to his knees, his worst fear was realized. Jessica was slumped over the fountain, her hair wet and matted to her face. He turned her on her back, and his heart lurched at the sight of her pale face, a bluish tint around her mouth.

Her breath was faint but present, so he hauled her up and wrapped his arms around her to give her the Heimlich. One jerk and water gushed from her mouth. She choked and coughed up more water, but she'd opened her eyes and moved on her own.

The deputy wasn't having the same kind of luck with the other woman. Even in the low lights, Finn could see the red mark around the woman's neck. Unlike Jessica, that woman had been strangled.

Two more deputies ran onto the scene, all of them chattering about a gun.

When Jessica stopped sputtering, Finn curled an arm around her shoulders. "Are you all right? The cops are here, but I don't know why or how they knew to come."

Jessica swiped an arm across her nose and mouth. "I called 911 on my way. Told them someone had a gun in the Art Garden. How's…"

Finn shook his head. "She didn't make it."

Jessica broke down, covering her face with her hands and sobbing, the sound hoarse and broken.

The first deputy on scene, who'd identified himself as Deputy Lorman, took control. "Everyone step back from the body."

Finn shouted, "We need an ambulance. Jessica almost drowned."

Lorman replied, "On it. I called for backup."

Jessica bent forward and Finn caught her before she could pass out on the cement, but she felt the ground with her hands. "My gun. Where's my gun?"

Aiming his phone's flashlight at the ground, Finn said, "He must've taken it. I didn't see a gun."

Jessica, her hand to her throat, said, "Get Detective Morse over here. This woman is another victim of the Kitsap Killer, or whatever you're calling him, and he probably took off toward the woods. He knows them well."

Finn turned toward Lorman. "Jessica's right. He had to have gone toward the woods. I was calling Jessica's name as I was running toward the fountain. I must've scared him off, but he didn't come at me, so he must've headed for the woods...unless he's in Callahan Hall."

Lorman's lips flattened into a grimace. "Do you know for sure it's the same guy who murdered Morgan and Missy, ma'am?"

"The killer texted me before he did it." She squeezed out her wet hair over one shoulder. "Or I don't know. Maybe he'd already killed her before he even texted me."

"Description? What was he wearing?" Lorman snapped his fingers at the two deputies guarding the scene.

"I don't know." Jessica shivered. "Gloves and black pants. That's all I saw. He came up behind me."

The deputies responded to Lorman's frantic finger snapping and stood at attention. The shorter one asked, "What do you need, sir?"

"One of you take the woods and the other, Callahan Hall. Check for wet footsteps, broken branches, open doors in the building. Black pants, black gloves. Go, do your jobs." He turned back to Jessica and Finn. "Do either of you know the dead woman?"

When Finn had come on the scene, he hadn't even looked at the girl's face—just the red marks on her neck. Now he peered over Jessica's shoulder at the figure crumpled on the ground.

As Lorman highlighted her face with his flashlight, Finn's eye twitched. He rose from his place beside Jessica and hunched forward. Then he swore.

Jessica clutched at his arm, too traumatized to turn and look, herself. "You know her?"

"That's one of my students—Gabby Medina."

As Finn sank back down, his head in his hand, sirens wailed through the air. This was going to be a long night.

JESSICA SAT ON the edge of the hospital bed swinging her legs. If Finn asked her one more time how she was feeling, she might just scream at him.

He'd insisted the EMTs take her to the hospital, even though she felt fine. The nurses had checked her vitals several times, listened to her lungs, her heart, and had given her intravenous electrolytes.

She was fine. Gabby Medina was dead.

Why her? Why was this person putting her through this? Could she have saved Gabby's life if she'd been faster? Smarter? Braver? Stronger?

That's exactly what Detective Morse wanted to know and had grilled her at the scene, despite Finn's protests. Morse wasn't done with her, either. He wanted her at the station tomorrow morning for the second interrogation. She didn't know what else she could tell him. She'd spilled her guts about the connections to Tiffany's murder—the card, the doll, the burglary of her sister's place and the stolen red scarf.

Morse had confiscated her phone, but she already knew the killer had used a different burner phone from the one he'd used the first time he texted her. Maybe Morse should start looking into who was buying up all the burner phones on Kitsap Peninsula.

Finn looked up from his phone. "Are you sure you're okay?"

Jessica ground her back teeth together behind a smile. The man had saved her life, after all. "I feel fine. Throat's a little raw from upchucking a gallon of water. Neck's sore from where he grabbed me. But I'm just ready to go back to the hotel."

One of the nurses must've been hovering outside because she chose that moment to push through the door. "Ready to leave, Jessica?"

Jessica hopped off the bed. "More than ready."

Forty-five minutes later, she got her wish as Finn wheeled into the parking lot of the hotel. He wouldn't let her drive her own car home.

He pulled into a parking space and cut the engine. "I'm coming up with you, and I'm staying the night. The nurse warned you might have some complications."

"She also mentioned that would be very rare, as you Heimliched all that water out of my lungs." His insistence had put her at ease, though. She didn't want to go to her room alone. Didn't want to spend the night alone. Didn't want to be alone ever again. "What about Bodhi?"

"I already called my neighbor. He probably had a game of fetch in the water, shared some dog food with the golden retriever next door and now they're both curled up in front of a crackling fire."

As they stepped into the lobby, the usually friendly desk clerk didn't even look up from his computer screen when she walked past him. She'd probably become the town pariah. Would Missy and Gabby even be dead if this guy hadn't wanted to somehow show off for her? That's all she could imagine he was doing. Why give her, of all people, a heads-up?

Once inside her room, Finn took charge. He pointed to the bathroom. "Wet clothes off. Take a warm shower. I'll make you some tea."

She followed his orders and grabbed her pajamas on her way to the bathroom. She shrugged off her damp jacket and peeled her sodden shirt from her body. Her jeans were just dirty, and she kicked those off, too.

The warm spray of the shower hit her face, and she jumped. The memory of her face in the fountain, the strong force pinning her down, had her doubling over. After everything, she hadn't actually feared the killer as he never seemed interested in harming her...until now.

She washed her hair and hurried through the rest of her shower. She slipped into her pajamas, a practical two-piece set, and ran a dryer over her hair, scrunching up her curls. True to his word, Finn had a cup of hot tea waiting for her on the nightstand.

He patted the bed. "Come over here and relax."

She appreciated his solicitousness, but she knew he had an ulterior motive—and it wasn't sex. He hadn't been present for most of her conversation with Detective Morse, and he wanted the rest of the details. She didn't blame him. She had questions of her own about Gabby Medina.

She crawled onto the bed, fluffed pillows behind her and sat cross-legged as she slid her hand around the paper cup of steaming tea. "Fire away."

"If you're not up to..."

She sliced a hand through the air. "We both know we need to debrief here."

Finn didn't waste any more time. "He texted you from a different number during the vigil. The text you forwarded to me—was that the first one?"

"No. The first text was that it was getting rowdy *here*. So I knew he was in the quad or had been in the quad. When I asked him, he answered that he had left with a friend.

And I knew then he was going to do something bad or had already done it. I fired off a million questions and he answered with the one I forwarded to you." She slurped the tea. "I really did try to get your attention before I went to the Art Garden."

"I believe you. The scene was crazy. I didn't even hear my phone ring. I did notice you leaving, though, and when I got that text, I figured it out."

"I had my weapon with me, which I no longer have. I should've gone in more aggressively, but when I saw that woman…when I saw Gabby, I lost it. He took advantage of that and attacked me." She tapped a fingernail against the paper cup and stared into her tea.

"What's wrong?"

"He attacked me. He's never done that before—the tires, the doll, even the discovery of Missy's body—he never tried to physically harm me."

"I hope you weren't sitting around thinking you were safe from this guy just because he spared your life a few times." He dropped onto the bed beside her, making her tea slosh in the cup. "He's a psychopath. Now he's a serial killer. He's not rational."

"I know, but why now? And why is he leading me to his fresh kills? It's sick. I hate it." She dropped her chin to her chest, and a tear rolled down her face.

"It has something to do with your sister's murder. Maybe he's a Plank fan. I know, I know. Maybe Plank didn't kill Tiffany, but most people believe he did. This guy believes Plank was responsible for Tiffany's murder, so he's involving you."

"I wish he'd stop." She dashed her wet cheek with the

back of her hand. "What about Gabby? Her name doesn't start with an *M*, but did she work on campus?"

Finn's eyes darkened and a muscle twitched at the corner of his mouth. "She worked at the ice cream shop. I saw her the day I talked to Deke. She popped her head into his office."

Jessica clapped a hand over her mouth. "Does Morse know this?"

"I told him everything."

"Those alibis. I hope the sheriff's department is going to recheck those alibis. Deke has a brother, right? Maybe it was his brother in that bar at karaoke night while Deke was murdering Morgan. Maybe they look alike. Tiffany and I didn't, but we had different fathers."

"I'm sure Morse is on it." He gave her a glance out of the corner of his eye. "He's on you, too. He's not happy the killer led you to two bodies."

"*He's* not happy?" She thumped her chest. "How does he think *I* feel? I didn't ask for this."

"You didn't see anything in the Art Garden?"

She drew her knees up to her chest, wrapping one arm around her legs. "I was so focused on Gabby's body, I didn't even hear him come up behind me until it was too late. I was right at the edge of the fountain, giving him a perfect opportunity. He rammed into me, pushing me into the water face-first. Before I got over my shock, he was holding my head down. I saw black jeans, felt a gloved hand on my neck. He was probably wearing a mask just in case he didn't successfully kill me."

"Didn't see any red scarf, hair color? Smells?"

"No, he wasn't wearing cologne or aftershave. Hadn't eaten any garlic or kimchi, either." She inhaled her tea before taking a sip. "I just don't understand why he tried to kill me."

"Uh, because he's a killer."

"You know what I mean." She yawned, the adrenaline of the evening finally dissipating. "I'm okay now. You can go home."

"There's no way I'm leaving you in this hotel room alone tonight." He got off the bed. "I can sleep on the sofa in the corner."

"With your legs draped over the edge?" She smoothed the covers beside her and then patted the bed. "If you're staying as my protector, you can sleep in the bed. It's not like we haven't shared a bed before."

"Yeah, and I remember how that ended." He toed off his sneakers. "I'll swish some of your toothpaste around in my mouth, and then I'll join you *on* the bed."

The terror of the night had buried any lustful inclinations she might have had about Finn for the moment, but his presence made her feel warm and safe—and sometimes warm and safe beat out lust by a mile.

As Finn took a step toward the bathroom, his cell phone rang on the nightstand. He pivoted. "This time it's my phone."

While handing it to him, she looked down at the display and swallowed hard. "Unknown number."

"Then I'd better take it." He plopped on the bed next to her and put the phone on speaker before answering it. "Who is this?"

A low voice hissed over the line. "It's your subject, Avery."

Jessica hugged herself. His voice sounded even more sinister over the phone.

"How'd you get your hands on a cell phone, Plank?"

"Come now, Professor. You know by now a con can get anything inside—for the right price. I call you after midnight and you're wondering how I got the phone?" Plank clicked his tongue. "You never stopped being a cop."

Finn met Jessica's eyes and rolled his own. "What do you want?"

"I heard all about the hijinks at Kitsap College tonight, Professor, and how Jessica Eller was involved...again."

Jessica scooted closer to Finn and twined her arm through his. She didn't like hearing her name on Avery Plank's lips, even over the telephone.

Finn's voice grew rough. "A woman was murdered, and another was almost murdered. I'd call it more than hijinks."

"Of course *you* would. To me it's a lark."

Finn growled low in his throat. "What do you want?"

"If you're still in touch with Jessica Eller, and I'm betting you are, you need to warn her."

Finn squeezed her thigh. "About what? She already knows this killer has a target on her back."

Plank chuckled. "I'm sure she does, but you'd better tell her to watch that target on her back very closely because I didn't kill her sister. That guy's still out there—and now it's personal."

Chapter Fourteen

Jessica's heart skipped a beat, and she dug her fingers into Finn's arm.

"How do you know this, Plank? What do you mean by personal? Has this guy been in touch with you? Is he a fanboy?"

"So many questions, Professor. I think I like you better when we're discussing your book about me, and I did just give you a nugget for that book, an exclusive. I did not kill Tiffany Hunt. You can tell her sister that bit of news, not that she ever believed I had killed her."

"You got that right, Plank." Jessica punched the pillow in her lap. "Now, how do you know so much about this guy?"

Plank said, "Oh, she's there."

Finn shook his head. Jessica knew he didn't want her talking to Plank, but she was tired of being afraid. "I'm here and I want answers. Why, other than the obvious, do you think these murders are some sort of personal message to me?"

"The first murder was to get you there, to get your attention. He copied your sister's killing—even if he wasn't responsible for that one. The second and third murders were to bring you glory."

She barked out a bitter laugh. "How did those murders bring me glory? They made me sick."

"The Kitsap Killer, as I believe he's now being called, let you find the bodies."

"*Let* me?"

Plank coughed and lowered his voice. "He was doing you a favor, Jessica. He knows your line of work. He figured giving you a heads-up on the murders would win you points the lab."

She snorted. "He doesn't know how the lab works. We're supposed to be investigating and analyzing evidence, not discovering it on our own."

Finn interrupted. "He didn't do her any favors tonight. He tried to kill her."

"Hmm." Sounded like Plank was tapping on the phone. "He didn't plan that. You must've done something to upset him. Did you call him a name? Try to humiliate him?"

"No." Jessica squeezed her eyes closed, replaying the moments when she approached the fountain with the gun pulled. "I had a gun, and I told him I'd called the cops. I *had* called the cops."

"Ahh." Plank released a noisy breath. "That's it. You betrayed him. He was sharing his kill with you, and you came with a gun intending to harm him, and you called the police. He reacted to that."

They could hear another voice in the background. "My turn."

"So sorry, Jessica, Professor. My time is up, but I'll be following the case of the Kitsap Killer—not as colorful as the Creekside Killer, though." Plank cleared his throat. "Now that you know I didn't kill Tiffany, maybe we can be friends, Jessica."

Jessica almost gagged. As she opened her mouth to return a nasty retort, Finn tapped her hand. He shook his head and ran a finger across his neck.

She gulped back her bile. "I don't know about being friends, but I do appreciate your input, and I'm glad to finally get confirmation that Tiffany's killer is still out there. So…thanks for that."

"Of course. If I have any more insight, I'll call you."

"Jessica doesn't have a phone. You can call me."

"Yes, Professor. You'll need to protect her."

Plank ended the call abruptly, and she and Finn stared at the phone on the bed.

She asked, "Is that what you do when you interview him for the book? You pretend to be his friend?"

"Avery Scott Plank is a psychopath. He doesn't understand the concept of friendship, so that's not necessary. It's a game to him. He's a smart guy. Don't underestimate him because he also happens to be evil." Finn drummed his fingers against the headboard. "What he said on the phone about the Kitsap Killer and you makes sense. You were just wondering why KK hadn't tried to harm you before last night."

"Why would he want to do me any favors? He doesn't owe me anything…unless he did kill Tiffany. I don't believe for a second he feels bad about that murder, but maybe in his warped mind he thinks he can make up for my loss by giving me the heads-up on his current crimes. Like you said, it's a game."

"Or he's taunting you."

"Taunting me?"

Finn jumped from the bed and paced to the window. "You couldn't save Tiffany. You were away at college, but you still blamed yourself. KK is giving you a chance to redeem yourself, but not really. It's just an illusion."

"Okay, Professor, you're losing me. Don't forget. I almost drowned tonight." She hit the side of her head with the heel of her hand. "My brain is probably waterlogged."

"Think about it." He raised one finger and took another hike across the room, as if on the stage in a lecture hall. "KK is providing you with an opportunity to save his victims. He contacts you minutes before he kills them, or so he says, giving you the false belief that if you got there quickly enough you could prevent their deaths. He's dangling that carrot. Holding out the possibility that you can right history. You couldn't save Tiffany, but you just might be able to save Missy or Gabby."

"Th-that's sick." Jessica folded her arms across her stomach. "He must be zeroing in on me because he killed Tiffany himself, or because, like you mentioned to Plank, he's captivated by my sister's case. Maybe he grew up here and knows the story. How does he know so much about me, though? That's what makes me think he's actually Tiffany's killer."

Clasping the back of his neck with one hand, Finn stopped his pacing. "Anyone fixated on Tiffany's case would know all about her ardent younger sister. You talked to the press frequently. You gave interviews. You made sure the world knew Tiffany Hunt had a sister and that sister was adamant about getting justice for Tiffany."

"Got me." Jessica rubbed her chin. "I also visited quite a few of those true crime chat rooms."

"You're kidding me." Finn plowed a hand through his hair, making it stand on end like a mad professor's.

"I'm afraid not." Jessica tried to make her voice small,

but the damning statement was out in the open. "I know that was ill-advised, but it seemed like a good idea at the time."

"When was the last time you logged on to one of those sites?"

She knew exactly when, but she rolled her eyes to the ceiling as if she had to think about it. "A few months ago."

"KK could've been in the chat rooms with you. I do a whole unit in one of my classes on these true crime discussion boards, blogs, podcasts. It might be worth checking back with the website to see if we can find any clues now that there's a copycat."

"Or the original." Jessica yawned.

Finn dropped to the edge of the bed and reached for her ankle, wrapping his fingers around it. "I was supposed to be staying here to watch over you and make sure you got some rest. Instead, you're over here talking to Plank and mulling over theories as to why a serial killer is harassing you."

Reclining against the pillows, she said, "Once I heard Plank's voice on the line, there was no way I *wasn't* going to speak with him, and talking to him is what engendered the theories." She picked up her paper cup and drained the remnants of her tea. "You brought me tea, though. You did good."

Finn turned off all the lights except for the lamp on his side of the bed. "I'm going to take a quick shower. Make sure you let me know at any time tonight if you're not feeling well. You're not out of the woods yet."

Finn closed the bathroom door behind him and as the shower started, Jessica crawled beneath the covers and flipped them back on Finn's side. He didn't have to sleep on the tiny sofa or the floor or the foot of the bed.

After the terror of the night, she wanted that man right

next to her. Although sex was the last thing on her mind, she trusted Finn. She trusted him with her life. She could trust him with her heart.

By the time he came back to bed, Jessica's lids drooped heavily over her eyes. He slid into bed beside her, his back toward her. She rolled to her side and wrapped one arm around his waist, burying her nose in the warm, slightly damp skin of his back.

She whispered, "Was Gabby a good student?"

"Bright, inquisitive, the best." Finn's voice was hoarse.

Tucking her hand in Finn's, she said, "Tell me we're going to catch this guy before he can destroy any more lives."

If Finn answered her, she didn't hear him. Instead, she pressed her face against his shoulder as a tear slid down her cheek.

THE FOLLOWING MORNING, Finn woke up with Jessica wrapped around his body—one arm flung over his chest and one long, smooth leg entwined with his.

He closed his eyes as he ran a hand over her wavy wheat-colored hair, and then rolled out of the bed, planting his feet on the floor. Jessica didn't need that sort of comfort right now.

He stalked off toward the bathroom to have a dip in a cold—or at least cool—shower. He squeezed some of Jessica's toothpaste onto his finger and ran it over his teeth—the next best thing to a toothbrush.

"Coffee?" Jessica tapped on the door. "I can either make a cup of instant in the room or order some room service."

"It's Sunday. Go ahead and order some breakfast from room service, unless you have someplace to be. I'd like to take a look at those true crime chat rooms. Been thinking about them all night." He swung open the door and kissed her on the mouth, showing off his new, minty breath. A man could only show so much restraint.

"So, not a good night's sleep for you?" Her gaze did a hungry inventory of his bare chest that weakened his restraint even more.

"Not great." *In so many ways.* "Why don't you get ready, and I'll order the breakfast."

"You got a deal." She slid open the closet and grabbed some clothes, and then they did an awkward dance in the doorway of the bathroom as they switched places.

"Are you an eggs and bacon kind of girl?"

"At this place, I'm a cinnamon swirl French toast kinda girl."

She retreated to the bathroom, and Finn got on the phone to order room service. Then he checked on Bodhi and pulled out his laptop.

The vigil last night had ended in chaos as word of another murder leaked. He'd had doubts that his female students would even make it to class next week. The president was making noise about switching classes online until the police could get things under control.

When the shower stopped, Finn tapped on the bathroom door. "Breakfast is on the way. What's the name of the most recent true crime site you visited?"

Jessica's muffled voice came through the door. "Cold Case dot com. We can access it on my laptop. I have an account with them, and the log-in is saved on my computer. Just give me a few more minutes."

Finn backed away from the door, trying not to picture

Jessica stepping out of the shower, rubbing a towel across her body. "Take all the time you need."

He went back to his computer and logged in to the teacher portal for Kitsap College and started entering the midterm grades. He'd done a good job of distracting himself, as he hadn't even noticed Jessica had entered the room until she came up behind him, touching his shoulder.

"Have you looked at any of the news about Gabby's murder?"

"Not this morning." A knock on the door interrupted them. "You can switch over to a news site while I get our breakfast."

He opened the door to a young guy gripping the handles of a cart laden with silver-domed dishes and a pot of coffee. "Good morning... Professor Karlsson."

"Morning." Finn cocked his head. His classes tended to be big, and he didn't always get to know his students.

"Uh, Jamie... Martin." He wheeled the cart into the room and said over his shoulder, "Had you for Criminal Investigations. Good class. I'm planning on law school."

Jessica glanced up and smiled.

As he parked the cart next to the table where Jessica pored over the laptop, Jamie's speculative gaze flickered from Jessica back to Finn.

At least Jessica was fully dressed, even down to her white sneakers. "Glad you got something out of the class."

Jamie started transferring the dishes from the cart to the table. "Did you really find Gabby's body last night?"

"I was on the scene, yeah." Finn shoved his hand in his pocket for some cash. "Did you know Gabby?"

"Not really. Saw her around." Jamie placed some cloth napkins and silverware on the table. "The women on campus are terrified. My girlfriend said she's not leaving her apartment. Are we going to online classes?"

"Maybe." Finn held out a generous tip, folded between his fingers. "Keep that girl of yours safe—and yourself, too."

Finn walked Jamie to the door and locked the top lock behind him.

Jessica picked up the coffee pot and poured two cups. "There isn't much online, but there might be a witness this time."

"That's good news. Did someone see something before or after the crime?"

"A woman thinks she saw Gabby walking away from the quad last night with a guy—dressed in black with a black hoodie."

"These kids wear hoodies like armor. Everyone walks around with their hoods up, hiding their faces. Was that the case with this man? Or woman, who knows?"

"Yes. She can't give any kind of description, other than the clothing, but that would match what I saw. Also, if she was calmly walking away from the vigil with this guy, she must've known him."

"After Deke Macy, the sheriff's deputies are questioning all the people who work on campus."

"That's a tall order." She tapped one cup of coffee with a spoon. "Cream? Sugar?"

"Thanks, I'll dump some cream in there." He lifted the lid from one of the plates and inhaled the sweet cinnamon aroma. "Now, that smells good."

Jessica rearranged the table, moving his laptop to the credenza and pulling out her own, which she set down next to the food. "I'll bring up the cold case website."

"Eat something first." He shoved her plate toward her. "How are you feeling this morning?"

"Physically, I'm fine. Emotionally?" She whipped the napkin into her lap and sliced a corner off the end of her French toast. "I'm a wreck. Sad, confused, still in shock. I can't believe what I witnessed last night. Can't believe we talked to Avery Plank."

"I hate to admit it, but he made a lot of sense." Finn dived into his bacon and eggs and helped himself to another cup of coffee.

Jessica picked at her French toast, plucked off some candied pecans and then shoved the plate toward him. "Try it."

As he plunged his fork into the cinnamon swirls, Jessica licked her lips and pulled her laptop in front of her. Her fingers tapped the keyboard and she whistled. "Celine, my PI, thinks she located my brother. I had ignored an email she sent a few days ago, so she sent me another."

"That's good." He waved a fork encrusted with sticky crumbs in her direction. "Any news about the case?"

"Nothing." She clicked the keys again and moved the laptop to share the screen with him. "Here's the website, Cold Case dot com."

"Why is your sister's case on here? It's not officially a cold case."

"There are a lot of cases like that—ones where there's doubt."

He raised an eyebrow at her. "You're not the only one with doubts?"

"No, I'm not." She signed into the website and selected a chat room from her saved favorites. She sucked in a breath. "Great minds think alike. There's been a lot of activity here the past few weeks. Those of us who doubted now see the connection between Tiffany's murder and the current homicides—and these people don't even know half of what I know."

Finn placed a hand over hers, hovering over the keyboard, fingers ready to type. "And they're not going to know what you know, right? Keep the card, the doll, the red fibers to yourself. You could compromise this investigation."

She flicked his hand from hers. "I know that."

Peering over her shoulder as she typed, he said, "Your profile name is jessiejames? He was an outlaw."

"Yeah, well, it's not easy thinking up original profile names." She skimmed through the messages. "Yep, yep. These online sleuths noticed the similarities between Tiffany's murder and Morgan's right away. Wow, they've even read about the witness who saw Gabby with someone last night. They're on top of things."

"Any of them ever solve a real crime?" Finn jabbed his finger at an envelope icon with red numbers on it in the upper-right corner of the window. "What's that?"

"Private messages. Members can message each other privately if they want to keep something out of the public chat room."

"Looks like you have messages."

"A lot of time it's personal requests, sometimes appeals for money that the moderators don't allow." The cursor skittered toward the envelope and Jessica clicked on it.

A string of messages appeared, all from the same user. Finn asked, "Do you know who TheHunter is?"

"Doesn't ring a bell." She double-clicked on one of the messages and gasped. "It's him, Finn. TheHunter is the killer."

Chapter Fifteen

A chill rippled down her spine as Jessica double-clicked the next message and the next and the next, all sent by The-Hunter, all implicating him as the Kitsap Killer, all pointing to him as Tiffany's killer.

"Slow down." Finn encircled her wrist with his fingers. "What is he saying here?"

Jessica took a big breath and clicked on the first message, sent four days earlier. "This one asks what I thought about the card. The next one asks about the doll."

"Is there any information on the message board about the card or the doll?"

"I-I'm not sure." She clicked away from TheHunter's personal messages back to the board. "I think the easiest way to find out is through a search. I can search the different threads."

She entered the word *doll* in the find field and clicked on the magnifying glass. Her stomach knotted when several threads popped up. "Oh my God. That information is being bandied about here. I swear I haven't even been on this website since the current murders."

Finn, trying to be the voice of reason, said, "The-Hunter just might be referring to the rumors on this message board."

"But why is he private messaging me? He calls himself TheHunter. Tiffany's last name was Hunt."

"Are you a frequent visitor to this board? Maybe he… or she sent private messages to other posters. TheHunter is just asking about those items, not claiming he left them. TheHunter could be referring to hunting clues or the truth." He nudged her fingers off the keypad. "Can we see who first mentioned these items?"

What Finn said made sense, but how would anyone on this website know about the card and the doll? As Finn searched, Jessica wrapped her hand around her cup and took a sip of lukewarm coffee.

"Here we go." Finn tapped on the screen. "A user by the name of Queenie posted something four days ago about a sympathy card mentioning Tiffany and a rag doll that you recognized as Tiffany's left at Morgan's memorial site. The-Hunter probably just got the info from the boards, but what about this Queenie person?"

Jessica smacked her hand on the table, rattling all the leftover breakfast dishes. "Queenie is Ashley King. Because of her last name, Tiffany used to call her Queenie. I told her and Denny about the card and the doll, and she turned around and blabbed about it on here."

Finn forked the last piece of French toast into his mouth. "There you go. Not optimal but not the killer."

"I'm not that easily convinced. I'm going to go comb through these message boards and find out what else Queenie and TheHunter have had to say in the past. Maybe Denny is the TheHunter."

"Before you do that, maybe you should read your boss's emails." He circled a finger around a message at the bottom of her screen. "That's about the third email notification from your boss that's popped up since we've been sitting here."

She sighed. "Why doesn't he just call me?"

"The sheriff's department has your phone, remember?"

She clicked on the three emails from Michael in succession, each plea for her to call him more demanding than the previous one.

"It sounds like he really, really wants you to call him." Finn slid his phone toward her. "Knock yourself out."

"I don't even have his number memorized." She hunched over the phone and tapped in the personal cell phone number at the bottom of Michael's email. "Voicemail. Hey, Michael, it's Jessica. I'm calling from a friend's phone, as you know very well mine was confiscated last night. You can call me back on this number."

She placed Finn's phone on the table and turned her attention back to the message board. "I'm going to go out and see Ashley again and ask her what the hell she's playing at. I'm pretty sure I told her not to tell anyone about what I'd found."

Finn's phone rang. "That was fast."

Stepping away from the computer to stretch, Finn said, "Help yourself, but you're going to need to get yourself a temporary phone."

"Hello, Michael. Before you rip into me about last night, I did call 911 on my way to the Art Garden, and the sheriff's department grilled me thoroughly. I gave them everything I had—including my phone."

"It's not about that, Jessica. Detective Morse relayed all that to me." He cleared his throat. "It's about that DNA sample, from the red fiber."

She waved one arm in the air to get Finn's attention,

and then tapped the speaker icon on his phone. "Is there a match? I thought we weren't sending it through CODIS yet."

"We're not, but there's an internal match."

Jessica's mouth dropped open. "Internal? You mean like someone in law enforcement?"

"The sample was a partial match to your sister's DNA—Tiffany Hunt."

"What?" Jessica put her hand on top of her head just in case it exploded. "The DNA is a match to Tiffany's? How can that be?"

Michael groaned. "I said *partial* match, which means it's yours, Jessica. You contaminated the evidence. You're off this assignment. You've been too distracted by this whole thing. You've insinuated yourself into this investigation, and now you've compromised it."

"That's not possible, Michael. I handled all the evidence with care."

"Really? Like the card and that doll? Those could've been important to this case, but no attorney worth his or her salt would ever allow that in a court of law." Michael's voice softened. "I know this has been hard on you, Jessica, but you need to take a step back for the integrity of this case and...your own safety. Take a few days off."

Michael wouldn't listen to her weak denials or excuses, so she ended the call with a half-hearted apology. She rapped on her forehead with her knuckles. "I can't believe I did that. Michael's right. I've been treating these cases like my own private investigation. I'm doing a disservice to those young women."

Finn rubbed a circle on her back. "Don't beat yourself up. Your boss is wrong. You didn't insinuate yourself into these crimes, the killer dragged you into them. Like you told Plank last night, you didn't ask for this. Anyone would be rattled."

"Ugh, I can't believe I left my DNA on crime evidence. That's Forensics 101."

"That's also why your DNA, and that of other CSIs and some law enforcement personnel's, is in a local database outside of CODIS. Those checks have to be run first to rule out the people who may have handled the evidence."

"It was so promising."

"But not surprising. The Kitsap Killer hasn't left his DNA yet, but he'll mess up at some point. He'll make a mistake. They all do."

"Yeah, remind me again how long the Green River Killer was at large?" Jessica fell across the bed, her legs hanging over the edge.

"More than twenty years, but you just visited his current domicile." Finn put away his laptop and stacked up the dishes on the tray. "I'll leave this out in the hallway on my way out. If you're okay, I need to get home and collect Bodhi and finish my grading."

"I'll be fine. Didn't you hear Michael? I'm on vacation." She propped herself up on her elbows. "Thanks for staying with me last night, even though…"

"There was nowhere else I wanted to be, even though…." He hitched his bag over his shoulder and strode toward the bed. Leaning over, he kissed her, just like he did this morning.

And just like this morning, the touch of his lips sent butterflies swirling in her stomach.

As he stopped at the door with the tray in hand, he turned and said, "Get yourself a temporary phone and call me later."

When the door slammed behind him, Jessica scrambled from the bed. She may be on forced vacation, but that didn't mean she had to stop working on this case. She'd been doing her best work on her own, anyway, and as far as she could tell—she was the closest person to catching the killer.

WHEN FINN HAD been gone almost an hour, Jessica pulled on a sweatshirt and grabbed her purse. She didn't have a phone to call Ashley and alert her to her visit, but maybe that was a good thing. Ashley acted as if she wanted Jessica to accept Plank's guilt in Tiffany's murder, but she hadn't moved on herself. *Queenie.*

Luckily, she remembered the way to Ashley's mobile home park. Did Denny have a username on the website, too? Were they both poking their noses into the investigations—past and present? She'd handed them two clues. Why didn't they tell her they were looking, too? Ashley pretended it was a done deal.

Michael hadn't mentioned any other DNA but hers on the red fiber, but maybe they couldn't separate anything else from hers. She'd messed up. Jessica sent a silent apology to Morgan, Missy and Gabby. And then she let out a not-so-silent scream in her car.

She hadn't been on the CSI team collecting evidence in the Art Garden. Detective Morse didn't want her there. Once the detective found out that she'd compromised the evidence in the other two cases, he would probably congratulate himself on the decision to keep her away. That was going to be a bitter pill to swallow in front of her colleagues at the forensics lab.

Jessica wheeled into the mobile home park and waved at a child on a tricycle. Pots of flowers and decorative trees brightened the yards of many of the mobile homes, which made Ashley's drab homestead stand out at the end of the row.

The inside of Ashley's place may be as chaotic as the place she'd shared with Tiffany, but Tiffany loved bright colors and beauty. If she lived with Ashley now, she would've turned the place into a charming, bohemian hideaway.

Jessica sniffed and parked the car in the same place as last time—behind a small white Toyota that had seen better days. At least she'd find Ashley at home this Sunday afternoon, unless she'd gone out with Denny. Jessica hadn't noticed Denny's car when she was here before.

She clomped up the two steps to the door. The mesh on the screen seemed to gape even wider than it had a few days ago. Ashley wasn't going to keep out many bugs, or even critters, with that thing.

The screen door protested when Jessica cracked it open to knock on the door. She stepped back and waited, listening for Ashley's heavy footfall on the floor inside. Instead, the tinny sound of the cheap TV chirped behind the door.

Jessica knocked again, harder. "Ashley? It's Jessica, Jessie, again. I need to talk to you."

She cocked her head, trying to filter out the background noise of the voices on the TV. "Ashley?"

Icy fingers trailed across her cheek, and she spun around. The kid on the trike had vanished, leaving her tricycle overturned in front of a mobile home with a swing set in front, one wheel spinning. A curtain twitched at the window of a home across the way, as a breeze rustled the crunchy leaves in Ashley's messy front yard and gave a silent push to the empty swing.

Jessica smacked her dry lips and knocked for a third

time. "Ashley, are you home? We need to talk about your posts on Cold Case dot com. I know you're Queenie on there. I'm not even mad. Please open the door."

Her last words came out on a desperate whine as her fingertips started to go numb. The hair on the back of her neck quivered as she crept down the porch steps and shuffled through the dead leaves to the front window.

"Ashley!" Jessica banged on the window, causing it to quiver. One half of the curtains were pulled too far to the middle, leaving a gap on the side.

Jessica sidled toward the edge of the window, cupped her hands over the glass and peered inside. She could see the end of Ashley's drab sofa. As her gaze focused, she could just make out Ashley lying on the floor of her living room, her head in a pool of blood. So. Much. Blood.

Chapter Sixteen

Finn careened toward the Fairwood Flats Mobile Home Park and slammed on his brakes outside the gates as he met a phalanx of emergency vehicles and a huge crowd of people. He'd never get through all of that, would never get to Jessica.

He spied the red hair of Detective Morse and threw his Jeep into Park as he scrambled out of his car. He'd been elbow-deep in grading all afternoon, but his buddy Zach had given him the heads-up about another dead body—once again discovered by Jessica Eller.

She was supposed to be on vacation.

He elbowed through the lookie-loos until he got to the crime scene tape, keeping the hordes at bay. He edged toward the deputy, one he didn't know, manning the perimeter.

"Hey, man. The woman who discovered the body is my…girlfriend. Can I duck under to make sure she's okay?"

"Sorry, Professor Karlsson. Nobody's going in or out except authorized personnel. I think Detective Morse is almost done questioning Ms. Eller. You shouldn't have to wait long to see her. She's fine." The deputy grimaced. "The other one, not so much."

At least the deputy knew who he was. That might not

gain him entrée into the magic crime circle, but it might get him something else. He dipped his head to the deputy's ear. "The other woman, Ashley King, right?"

The deputy nodded once, his gaze darting around to make sure nobody saw him talking to Finn.

Finn whispered, "Strangled like the others?"

"That's the thing." Quick glance over Finn's shoulder. "She was beaten to death with a blunt object."

Finn's gut knotted. The Kitsap Killer had wanted to distinguish this murder from his others. He had to know that killing Ashley King would connect him to Tiffany Hunt's murder, especially with Plank disavowing his previous confession. Maybe he didn't care. Maybe he was ready to take credit for that ten-year-old murder.

Had he called Jessica to the scene again? There's no way she would've come here on her own this time—not after what happened last night and her boss reading her the riot act about mishandling evidence. Besides, Jessica didn't have her phone. How would he have contacted her?

When Morse shifted positions, Finn caught a glimpse of Jessica, her blond hair hanging around her pale face, her arms crossed over her chest, shoulders hunched. It took every ounce of control and reason he had to stay behind the yellow tape and not go charging over there and take her in his arms.

He shuffled out of the crowd and sank down on an upright log that functioned as a barrier to the mobile home park. From his perch, he kept an eye on Jessica as she answered Morse's questions.

After almost thirty minutes, he sprang up from his log when a deputy led Jessica to a waiting patrol car. They weren't done with her. They were taking her to the station for questioning.

Even better. He could wait for her there.

He followed the deputy's patrol car to the station, joining a caravan of other vehicles, including a few news vans. By the time he parked at the station and exited his Jeep, the deputies had already hustled Jessica inside the station.

Finn walked inside and leaned over the front desk. "I'm here to pick up Jessica Eller when she's done."

The deputy on duty answered, "Noted."

While he waited for Jessica, Finn scanned through the news of the murder on his phone. Jessica's name hadn't been reported yet, so some stories were not linking Ashley's death to the current homicides. None of the outlets had mentioned the cause of death yet. Would the beating throw them off the scent of the Kitsap Killer? Fairwood hadn't had a murder in over five years. How coincidental would it be for a couple of killers to snap at the same time—unless Ashley's murder was personal.

How long before some enterprising journalist discovered that the Creekside Killer murdered Ashley's roommate ten years ago? How long before someone other than law enforcement would start piecing together the links between the murders? Everyone still believed Avery Plank had murdered Tiffany Hunt, but he could blow that truth right out of the water. Finn hadn't even told the police what Plank had admitted to him and Jessica. Would Plank backtrack from that admission?

He jerked his head up at the sound of footsteps in the back and half rose to his feet when he heard Jessica's voice.

"That's okay. I can get a ride back to Fairwood Flats."

Finn strode toward the front desk to meet her. "You don't need to do that."

Raising her chin, her eyes widened. "Finn."

A deputy, not Morse, stuck out his hand to Jessica. "Thank you again for your time, Jessica. If we have anything else, we'll let you know. Call us with your new number when you get it, if we don't release your phone first."

"Will do, Deputy Harris." Her pace picked up, and as she met Finn, she said, "Let's get out of here."

Harris pointed down the hallway from which they just emerged. "You can go out the back if you like. The press is still out front. By now, they probably know it's you who found the body."

Harris's implied "again" hung in the air as Finn took Jessica's arm. "Thanks, sir, we'll do that."

They did a 180 and made their way to the back door through the station. Before they exited, Finn draped his jacket over her shoulders, tugging the hood over her blond hair, just in case some sharp-eyed newshound noticed them sneaking to his car. They didn't exchange one word until Finn was behind the wheel and driving away from the station.

Shifting his gaze to the side, he said, "Dinner? Glass of wine? Bottle of wine?"

"I could use some food." She slumped in the passenger seat as he cruised past a news van with a reporter in front on a microphone. "This is already a circus, and they don't know the half of it."

"Neither do I."

She shook the hood from her head. "How'd you know where to find me?"

"As soon as I found out about Ashley's death and that

you were the one who found her, I raced to the mobile home park. The deputy on guard wouldn't let me past the tape, but I saw Morse talking to you. Then I saw him lead you to a patrol car and followed you to the station." He clasped her hand. "What happened? The Kitsap Killer didn't lure you out there again, did he?"

"No, although I'm not sure Morse or my boss Michael believe that." She tapped on the window with her knuckle. "They're probably not going to allow me to get my car just yet. Can we go to that restaurant near my hotel? Dockside Fish Grill?"

"Patio should be a private place to talk."

"He did it. I know he killed Ashley." She set her jaw. "I just don't know why."

"What brought you back to Ashley's?" He hit the steering wheel with the heel of his hand. "You were going to confront her about posting as Queenie."

"Of course. I wanted to know why she'd been pretending with me that she believed Tiffany's case was closed while posting clues on a discussion board."

"Maybe it was the stolen scarf. She could've heard about red fibers found at the crime scenes and started putting things together." Finn swung a U-turn and parked a block down from the restaurant.

There were a few more diners outside this time, but they still nabbed a table on the edge of the patio overlooking the water.

As Finn sat across from Jessica, he asked, "Do you want to tell me what you saw? Don't if it's going to upset you."

"I honestly didn't see that much." She downed half a glass of water before continuing. "I knocked on her door a few times. Heard the TV and got an uneasy feeling. I went around to the front window and saw her lying on the floor in a pool of blood. I must've screamed because a couple of neighbors rushed outside. One of them called 911. I didn't even know what had happened to her until Morse told me someone hit her on the head with a heavy object. They haven't identified the murder weapon yet. Nothing left there with blood or hair on it. I didn't even know if she was dead, although it sure looked like it." She punched a fist into her palm. "Why? Why target Ashley at this late date? She couldn't tell the cops anything last time, and she knows nothing about the current murders."

"Where was Denny?"

The waitress interrupted them, and they ordered their food and drinks.

"I don't know where Denny is. Thank God I didn't find his body, too." She chewed her bottom lip. "I hope he's okay."

"They might be looking at him for Ashley's murder." Finn held up a finger as Jessica opened her mouth. "Think about it. This is his second murdered girlfriend. What are the odds? The police don't have anything to tie Ashley to the Kitsap Killer slayings. She's not a student, doesn't work on campus, didn't know the victims."

"She was Tiffany's roommate."

"And Denny was her boyfriend. I'm just throwing him out there as a suspect. You know they'll be looking at him." He thanked the waitress for his beer and waved off the icy mug. "How are you doing? Take a sip of your wine. Maybe it'll put some color back in your cheeks."

She pressed a hand to her face. "Do I look that bad?"

"You look tired and frazzled and a little green around the gills. Did Morse and Deputy Harris grill you?"

She followed his advice and took more than a dainty sip from her glass. "What do you think? They suspected that the Kitsap Killer had given me another exclusive, like I'm a freakin' reporter instead of a forensics analyst. Michael, my boss, got in on the fun, too, calling the station while I was there for further questioning."

"Did you tell them about the Cold Case website and Ashley's posts? TheHunter's private chats?"

"I told them all of that." She swept her glass over the table, and her white wine sloshed inside dangerously. "I think I lost them at Queenie."

"I'm sorry, Jessica. I think you need to back away for a while."

"You're probably right, and Michael just extended my involuntary vacation, but I can't help thinking I'm the only one who can crack this. The Kitsap Killer is reaching out to me for some reason—whether or not he killed Tiffany. He's taking risks by contacting me. He left his comfort zone by murdering Ashley. He's going to make a mistake."

"If he does, Detective Morse will catch it. Let the police handle this. If you had shown up at Ashley's while he was there—" Finn shook his head "—he's already shown he's willing to hurt you to protect himself."

"I know you're right. You're all right. I'm going to give it a rest tonight and email the PI about my brother instead. She must've thought I lost interest."

The food arrived, and Jessica busied herself with tossing dressing into her crab salad and asking for another glass of wine. At least her appetite had returned, and she'd lost the haunted look around her eyes.

She even stole some fries from his plate, and he pretended to object.

As they finished their meal, Finn checked his phone. He still had grading to finish and online classes to plan.

Holding up his phone, he said, "We should've stopped before dinner to pick up a new phone for you. Everything will be closed now."

"I think I'm good." She drained the dregs of her second wineglass. "Deputy Harris indicated I could have mine back as early as tomorrow."

"Did they find out anything about the phone that texted you?"

"They were able to track the texts to one temp phone purchased in Los Angeles and another purchased in St. Louis, but they haven't gotten any further than that. The text messages I received were from two different phones, and he probably has another."

"And he most likely didn't buy them himself." Finn tossed his napkin on the table.

"Anyway, they have all the info from my phone that they need, so I'll probably get mine back tomorrow."

"Are you going to be okay at the hotel on your own tonight?" He crossed his arms and leaned on the table. "I hate to abandon you, but I have to finish my grading and set up my classes for the week, which are all online now. The president of Kitsap College sent out the message today."

"I'll be fine. I'm going to email Celine, my PI, and watch some TV. I'm officially on vacation."

"Yeah, you were officially on vacation today, too." He tipped his head at the waitress to get her attention. "And you probably shouldn't pick up your car tonight after those two glasses of wine."

"I was just thinking the same thing, not that I could pick

it up anyway. Who knows how much longer the sheriff's deputies are going to be at Ashley's."

"How are they supposed to contact you if they need to?" He pulled a credit card from his wallet and handed it to the waitress as she approached with the bill.

"I'm not in the middle of the wilderness. I do have a telephone in my room. I gave them my hotel. If they want to find me, they will. They're cops."

Once Finn settled the bill, he drove Jessica to her hotel and walked her all the way up to her room. He even stood outside her door until he heard the lock.

It's not that he didn't trust her to stay put. He didn't trust the Kitsap Killer. For whatever reason, this maniac had put a target on Jessica's back—and he was ready to hit the bull's-eye.

THOSE TWO GLASSES of wine had hit the spot. Jessica's neck and jaw didn't feel so tight, and her mind had stopped clicking. She pulled off her boots, gathered her hair in a ponytail, brushed her teeth and splashed some water on her face.

She studied her face in the mirror. Finn had been diplomatic. She looked a lot worse than tired and frazzled. She'd become Fairwood's pariah. She just couldn't shake the stench of death surrounding her.

She unplugged her laptop and carried it with her to the bed. She ran her hand over the smooth pillow beside her. Housekeeping had changed her bedding today and with that, swept away any traces of Finn's scent from the pillow.

Her attraction to him remained strong, despite all the turmoil in their lives—her life. He'd been there for her through every disaster—and it had required no manipulation from her. He wanted to be with her, to protect her.

That had been a hard concept for her, and Tiffany, to understand. Mom had used every tool of manipulation in the book to ensnare men, but they never stuck around. Jessica had never even met her father. He'd wanted nothing to do with Mom—or her. Tiffany's father had died before Tiffany tracked him down.

Her father might not want any contact with her, but apparently her brother had shown some interest. She flipped open her laptop and accessed her email. She vowed to stay off the cold case crimes website...for now.

She double-clicked on Celine's email. Seems her brother was skittish after hearing bad things about his family but might be interested in meeting her—and his other sister. Celine explained that she hadn't thought it was her place to tell him his other sister was dead. What a way to start off a new family relationship.

She dragged the hotel phone onto the bed and called Celine's number.

"Celine Jerome, private investigations."

"Hi, Celine. This is Jessica Eller. I got your email."

"It's about time, girl. I sent that a few days ago, and I've been trying to call you on your cell phone."

"I know, sorry. I've been busy...with work, and my phone isn't working."

"Understood." Celine shuffled some papers. "Good news is, I found your half brother, and he lives in Seattle, believe it or not. The bad news is, he's not absolutely sure he wants to establish contact. He's happy, he's settled."

"Wow, Seattle. I may have already met him in some capacity. I get that he might be leery." Jessica twisted her ponytail around her hand. "And I haven't even gotten to the part where his other half sister was murdered. Once I tell him that, he may just go running for the hills."

"He might. I know you've been anxious to meet him, but I wanted to check with you before giving him your contact info. He wants to be the one to make the first move."

"That's fine. I do want to meet him. In fact, I'd welcome the distraction about now. I'm not going to have my cell phone back and working until sometime tomorrow, but you can give him my cell number and my email address. Give him my work email, too. He might feel more comfortable if he sees I work for the Washington State Patrol. H-how does he sound?"

"Haven't spoken to him, and he doesn't want me to tell you his name, but our text exchanges have been good—no anger or outrage that you hired a PI to track him down. Seems cool."

"Great. I could use some cool right now. Go ahead and give him my details and tell him to reach out any time. And thank you so much, Celine. Send me your final bill."

"Don't thank me yet. He might decide to forgo the relationship. Like I said…jumpy."

"That wouldn't be your fault. I'm sure you told him what a spectacular person I am."

Celine chuckled. "I didn't, but you are. Take care."

When Jessica ended the call, she placed the receiver in the cradle. Celine's tone had changed at the end. Had Celine already read about her issues here in Fairwood? Once her half brother knew about those, he really wouldn't want to have a relationship with her.

As she put the phone back on the nightstand, a fire alarm in the form of unremitting beeps filled the room. Jessica jumped from the bed and poked her head into the hallway.

One door opened at the end, and Jessica shouted "Is this for real?"

The woman yelled back, "Not taking any chances."

Sighing, Jessica shoved her feet into her boots and zipped them up. She sniffed the air. She didn't smell any smoke, so she left her laptop, grabbed her purse and a jacket, and left her room.

She passed the elevator and pushed open the door to the stairs. As the woman down the hall had said, why take any chances. Luckily, no high-rise buildings were allowed in Fairwood, including hotels, so she had just three flights of stairs to navigate.

At the bottom, she shoved open the fire door that opened onto a side parking lot and sucked in the cool air. She ambled around to the front of the building. Other hotel guests and employees were scattered around the front of the building.

She spied the front desk clerk and made a beeline toward him. She didn't even have to ask her question, as he addressed a small clutch of people vying for his attention.

Raising his hands, he said, "I don't know if there's actually a fire in the hotel or not, but when the fire alarm goes off, everyone needs to evacuate and stay outside until the fire department comes, checks things out and gives us the all-clear signal. I'm sorry for the inconvenience. There are a few restaurants down the road still open, and you're welcome to enjoy our beautiful dock on the bay while you wait."

The sun had already set, but Jessica had grabbed her jacket on the way out, so she hugged it around her body and crossed the road to the water. She didn't want to clomp all the way out to the dock, and she didn't want to dangle her feet in the water again, so she clambered onto a pile of rocks that stood sentry on either side of the dock.

She brushed a layer of sand from the flat of one of the boulders and sat down. Closing her eyes, she focused on the sound of the water lapping against the wooden pilings of the dock.

Sand scuffled behind her, and she whipped her head around, almost colliding with a man's leg. When she opened her mouth to scream, he fell against her back and clamped a rough hand over her mouth.

Chapter Seventeen

She wasn't going down without a fight this time. She drove her elbow back, connecting with a kneecap.

The man grunted and his hand loosened on her mouth. She bit into the fleshy part of one finger, gritty with sand.

He yelped. "Ow! Jessica, let go. It's me, Denny."

She unclenched her teeth and spit into the sand. Then she jumped up from the rock and spun around, her fists raised.

Denny flinched and flapped his hand. "That hurt like hell. I think you broke the skin."

She snarled. "Good! What the hell are you doing sneaking up on me and covering my mouth? You're lucky my gun was stolen." Glancing over his shoulder at the hotel parking lot, Denny tucked his scruffy hair behind his ear. "I didn't want you screaming."

"You could've called my name first."

"Like I said, I didn't want you screaming." He flipped up his hood. "People think I killed Ashley. Do you think I killed her?"

"You're not a suspect, Denny. You're a person of interest. As far as I know, the police don't have any evidence against you, but you are…were her boyfriend and lived there with her. They need to talk to you."

"Yeah, they're gonna talk to me, all right. 'Your girlfriend was murdered ten years ago, Denny, and now you have another murdered girlfriend. Explain that while we lock you up.'"

Her breath returning to normal, she wedged her hands on her hips. "Did you pull the fire alarm in the hotel?"

"That was me." He patted his scrawny chest. "I knew you were staying at this hotel. Saw you go out with that cop."

"He's not a cop."

"Whatever. I knew that desk guy wasn't going to give me your room number, and I didn't want to give him my name." He hunched his shoulders. "I figured the fire alarm would get you outside where I could talk to you."

Narrowing her eyes, she asked, "Where were you when Ashley was murdered?"

"See? You think I did it."

"It's a simple question, Denny."

"I was in my rig on the outskirts of town. Me and Ashley had a spat." He sniffed and rubbed his nose. "She told me to take a hike, so I slept in my rig and I was still there."

She had to admit, his story was weak. "What was the fight about?"

"Other women. Always about other women."

Her gaze wandered from his bleary eyes to his stubbled chin down to his dirty jeans and scuffed boots. Real ladykiller. "Did she threaten to kick you out?"

"Nothing like that, but it's what she said before, Jessie. She was scared—not of me."

"Scared of what?" Jessica watched a couple of fire engines pull into the hotel parking lot, their sirens wailing. She could always make a run for it if Denny turned violent…or she could probably take him out herself.

"Some guy." Denny picked up a rock and skipped it into the bay. "She told me she'd seen the same guy in town who'd met with Tiffany years ago. She saw him for the first time yesterday. They met eyes, and she recognized him and realized that he knew she'd recognized him."

"What guy is this?" She snapped her fingers. "Ashley did mention someone she thought might've stolen the doll and scarf, but she said he left town before Tiffany was murdered."

"That's right. She told the cops about him at the time, but she didn't know his name or where he lived. He just showed up one day, hung out with Tiffany a few times and left. Tiff never introduced him to us. I never even saw him, but Ashley saw them together drinking coffee one day. She never saw him again—until yesterday, the day she was murdered."

"You think he killed Ashley because she recognized him."

"Yeah. I put two and two together. That's the only thing that makes sense to me." Denny covered his face with his hands, and his shoulders shook.

"I'm so sorry, Denny." Jessica rubbed his back. "Ashley was the sweetest person. I hope I didn't… I mean I hope my visit didn't draw the killer's attention to her."

He dragged his arm across his face. "That's not it, Jessie. It was that man. I'm telling you, Ashley was terrified."

"You need to go to the police, Denny. Tell Detective Morse everything you told me."

"What if this guy comes after me? What if he thinks Ashley told me or that I remember him? I don't. I don't."

"The police can protect you, Denny. This is important information they need to know."

"Like they protected Morgan, Missy and Gabby?" He took a cigarette from his pocket, which trembled as he held it between two fingers. "I don't think so. Just stay safe, Jessie. You don't even live in Fairwood. If you're done with your work, go back to Seattle." He squeezed her hand and turned away.

She watched Denny's dark figure climb over the rocks, the glowing light of his cigarette bobbing with each move.

Was she done with her work? She was done with her official work, but the unofficial work had consumed her and now Denny had handed her another clue. She owed it to Tiffany to follow up. She owed it to Morgan, Missy, Gabby and Ashley, too.

FORTY-FIVE MINUTES LATER, the fire department had given the all-clear signal, and Jessica shuffled back inside the hotel with the other guests, quite a few a little tipsy from their forced evacuation. The effects of her two glasses of wine had completely evaporated, and her nerve endings tingled anew after her encounter with Denny.

When she got to her room, she reached for the phone to call Finn and tell him all about this new piece of information. As soon as she picked up the receiver, she dropped it—and not because she hadn't memorized Finn's number, which she hadn't. If she ran to Finn with Denny's theory about the mystery man, Finn would only remind her to step back and leave it to the police.

And he wouldn't be wrong.

Instead, she got ready for bed and slipped between the covers, the TV remote on one side of her and her laptop on the other. She selected a reality TV show from the menu and pulled the computer into her lap. Without her phone, her email had become her only connection to the outside world.

Several new emails loaded, and she started with the oldest, a message from Celine with her final invoice and the news that she'd sent Jessica's contact info to her brother.

Jessica switched to her bank's website and sent Celine the money. Back to her email, she skimmed through a message from Michael reminding her to fill in her time sheet with her *vacation days*, as he still insisted on calling them. She had a different name for it—a forced leave of absence.

She clicked on the newest message from armybrat, an unknown email address. Excitement fizzed through her veins when she read the message. It was from her brother, and he'd signed the email with his name—David.

An image invaded her mind, and she squeezed her eyes closed to focus on a scene with a baby, almost a toddler, in a bouncy seat and a little girl with blond curls waving at him and giggling and chanting. "Wavy Davy, Wavy Davy."

Her lids flew open. Is it possible David had kept the same name Mom had given him? She'd remembered his name was David or maybe Tiffany told her that, but this was the first time she remembered the nickname she'd given him—Wavy Davy.

A tear trembled on the edge of her eyelash as she smiled. He wanted to meet her, but he had reservations, and he only wanted to meet one sister at a time. The tear dropped to her cheek and rolled down to her chin where it quivered before splashing onto the laptop. He'd never have that pleasure.

Her fingers hovered over the keyboard as she composed an email to the brother she hadn't seen in over twenty-five years.

THE NEXT MORNING all through breakfast, Jessica could hardly eat due to the butterflies in her stomach, but for a change these butterflies signaled excitement instead of fear. After exchanging several emails with David last night, they'd agreed to meet for dinner down in Kingston, as he'd be in Edmonds today and could take the ferry over. She felt giddy that she could complete one of Tiffany's dreams for her.

The hotel phone startled her, and she crossed the room to answer it, the butterflies turning into knots. "Hello?"

"It's Finn. How are you this morning? I regretted leaving you after dinner, but I figured you'd fall asleep right away."

"Not quite." She proceeded to tell him about the fire alarm and Denny's warning.

Finn swore. "Did Denny tell the police?"

"He's trying to avoid the police, but I'm going to mention it to them when I drop by the station today to get my phone."

"My first class starts in about an hour, but I called to see if you need a ride to pick up your car."

"No, I'm good. I can get there on my own. Then I'm going to see if I can get my phone." She paused. "I made contact with my brother last night."

Finn asked, "How'd that go?"

"Better than I expected. He's kind of guarded, and I still have to tell him about Tiffany."

"What's his name?" Finn had an edge to his voice.

"David, and he lives in Seattle. We're meeting for dinner tonight in Kingston."

"What's his last name?"

She cleared her throat. "H-he didn't reveal that to me. Like I said, skittish."

"Or weird. Why doesn't he want to tell you his last name?"

"Calm down. Celine vetted him. Remember, I reached out to him, not the other way around."

"Where's the dinner?"

"A restaurant called Salty Girls. He let me pick, and I figured that was appropriate as both Tiffany and I were salty girls." She checked the time on her laptop. "I need to run. I'll give you a call before I leave for Kingston, hopefully from my recovered cell phone. Good luck with those online classes."

She made her next call to the sheriff's station. When the deputy at the front desk answered, Jessica identified herself and asked if she could retrieve her car from in front of the crime scene at Fairwood Flats Mobile Home Park. When he gave her the okay, she traipsed down to the front desk to call a taxi. She couldn't even order a car without her cell phone. She should've asked that deputy if she could get her phone, too.

Fifteen minutes later on the taxi ride to Ashley's mobile home, the driver twisted in his seat as he pulled out of the hotel parking lot. "You heard about that murder out there."

"Yeah, terrible." Jessica clapped her sunglasses on her face and turned her head to stare out the window. She should follow Denny's lead and try to cover up so people wouldn't recognize her. Luckily, this driver just seemed to be sharing gossip with a fare.

When they arrived, she had the driver drop her off at the entrance to the mobile home park. She didn't want him dropping her off in front of a mobile home ringed with crime scene tape.

The deputies hadn't removed the yellow tape yet, but

none of it circled her car. She crept up to the driver's-side door, her head turned away from Ashley's place.

As she grabbed the door handle, a woman across the way looked up from her gardening and gave Jessica a hard stare. Jessica yanked open her door, dropped onto the seat and cranked on the engine. Denny had been right—she needed to leave this town. As soon as Deputy Morse gave her the go-ahead, she was out of here.

She'd lost her sister, but she had a brother. She needed to let Tiffany go and concentrate on forging a new relationship with David. Tiffany would've approved. Being the oldest sister, Tiffany had missed Wavy Davy more than Jessica had. Jessica had just been about three years old when child services took David away from Mom. Tiffany had been twelve, already too old for her years—a childhood lost.

Jessica drove straight to the sheriff's station from the mobile home park. Even though her forensics services were no longer needed or wanted on the case, she still had business to conduct.

She sailed through the front doors of the station like the frequent flyer she'd become. The deputy at the front desk, asking if she needed help, sounded like the same one who'd answered the phone earlier.

"I'm Jessica Eller. Detective Morse confiscated my cell phone for evidence, and he indicated yesterday that I might be able to pick it up today. Do you know if it's ready?"

The deputy picked up the phone. "Let me check with Deputy Lorman. He's in charge of that evidence from that case."

Lorman must've picked up because the front desk deputy started explaining the who, what, when to someone on the other line. He eyed Jessica as he nodded. "I see. Uh-huh. Yeah, I'll let her know."

Jessica raised her eyebrows when the deputy ended the call.

"I'm sorry, Ms. Eller. He's not ready to release your phone yet. Maybe later this afternoon or tomorrow."

"Ugh." She sawed her bottom lip with her teeth. Should she go through the trouble of getting a pay-as-you-go phone or not? She could touch base with David via email before she left, just to confirm. And she could always call Finn from the hotel phone. Her car had a GPS for the drive down to Kingston, not that she didn't know the way to Kingston, and she could plug the restaurant into her GPS.

"I'll get it tomorrow." She pointed to the phone. "Is Deputy Lorman available or Detective Morse? I have some information about the King homicide."

"They're both busy right now, out in the field. Unless you know who did it, you can probably give them a call and leave a voicemail. They both check in regularly."

"I'll do that." Denny was right. The investigation team probably wouldn't put much stock in anything Denny had to say—until they could get their hands on him to question him.

She spent the rest of the afternoon on errands and finishing up her work on Morgan's case, if Michael would accept it. Before she got ready for her dinner with David, she left Detective Morse a voicemail, left another message for Finn, who hadn't picked up, and sent an email to David to confirm.

When she emerged from the shower, the only one who had bothered to respond was her brother. All set.

She dressed casually in a pair of jeans, a green blouse,

a caramel-colored blazer and low-heeled boots to match. She'd discovered a spot of ketchup on the green sweater she told David she'd be wearing, but she didn't bother to update him. He said he'd be wearing glasses and a gray jacket. She'd find him. Would she know him anywhere?

She set the GPS in her car for Kingston and took off, her palms a little sweaty on the wheel. Was David as nervous as she was? The thirty-five-minute drive took her away from the coast and through a long stretch of greenery. When she passed the casino, she knew she was close.

Once she reached the town of Kingston, she spotted the red clapboard in front of the Salty Girls restaurant. Jessica pulled into the small parking lot on the side of the building and flipped down the visor to freshen her lipstick.

She walked into the restaurant and craned her neck to scan for any single guys sitting at a table. A man in glasses with brown hair half rose from his chair and lifted his hand.

A grin stretched Jessica's mouth as she approached her brother's table. When she reached it, he stood up fully and extended his hand and then dropped it when she moved in for a hug.

They gave each other one of those awkward one-armed clasps, and she laughed self-consciously. "David, finally. It's good to finally meet you."

"You, too. It's been a long time." He gestured to the seat across from him.

As Jessica sat down, she tilted her head. "Have we met before?"

FINN TRIED JESSICA's hotel number one more time, a kernel of unease lodged in his throat. He didn't like the idea of her meeting a stranger, for all intents and purposes, a stranger in another town with no cell phone.

Kingston wasn't that far, and she'd told him the name of the restaurant. He could always do a reconnaissance mission to spy on her and her brother. She'd be angry if she spotted him, though.

He blew out a long breath. He'd finished all his grading yesterday, and the online classes had gone better than expected. The young women in his class were relieved to be able to stay at home.

He'd get some dinner, do some research for his book and wait for Jessica to give him the report on her brother. He wanted her to leave Fairwood for now, but this time he didn't plan to let her disappear from his life. He hoped she felt the same way. He thought she did.

As he opened his fridge door to investigate what he could make for dinner, his cell phone rang. Spinning the phone around on the counter, he saw a number from the Washington State Patrol on the display. He grabbed it and tapped to answer. "Hello?

"Is this Finn Karlsson?"

"Who wants to know?"

"Sorry. This is Michael Wilder from the Washington State Patrol Forensics Division. I'm Jessica Eller's boss."

"Yeah, I know who you are. Are you trying to reach Jessica?"

"I am, yeah. It's important. When Deputy Lorman took her phone, she gave me your number."

"She went out to dinner."

Wilder swore under his breath. "I really need to talk to her. It's...well, it's her safety at stake here."

Finn had been hunched over the counter, but Wilder's

words had him snapping to attention. "I know where she is. I can get to her. What's going on?"

"She probably told you how she contaminated the DNA evidence on that red fiber, right?"

"Yeah, yeah. She told me all about it. Felt incredibly stupid, too."

"Well, it wasn't her fault. She *didn't* contaminate the sample."

Finn's heart pounded in his chest. "What do you mean? That wasn't her DNA from the sample?"

"The forensics techs jumped the gun. It was just a trace, a sample, and it partially matched right away to Tiffany Hunt's sample on file. The techs made an assumption before running additional tests on the sample. Once they ran further tests, they discovered it couldn't be Jessica's DNA."

Finn tried to swallow, his throat sandpaper. "Why couldn't it be a match?"

"Oh, it's still a partial match, but the DNA can't belong to Jessica because it belongs to a male. The trace DNA from the red fiber belongs to a male relative of Jessica's— like a brother."

Chapter Eighteen

Her brother smiled, and her heart skipped a beat at how similar it was to Tiffany's smile. He said, "It's funny. I feel the same way—like I've seen you before."

"It's more than that." She shook her head. "It's your voice…and your smile is so much like Tiffany's."

"I'm glad you see the resemblance." He put his hand over his heart. "You can tell her you found me, but I'm not ready to meet everyone yet."

Jessica swallowed and smiled too brightly. "I can understand that.

"So, tell me all about yourself." She planted her elbows on top of the table, ignoring the menus, and sank her chin in her palm. "What does your email name, armybrat, mean? Was your adoptive father in the army? Did you move around a lot?"

"Whoa! Slow down." Chuckling, he held up his hands and crossed one finger over the other. "My father was in the army, retired now, so I followed in his footsteps like a dutiful son. Spent some years in the army myself. Honorable discharge, got my teaching credential, thanks to the GI Bill, and found a job in Seattle. The Pacific Northwest always called to me."

"That's good. I'm glad life worked out well for you. Our sister—" Jessica chewed on the side of her thumb, not ready to spill the beans about Tiffany yet "—she had some issues as an adult. Chaotic childhood."

He dipped his head. "That's sad, but you turned out okay."

Jutting out her chin, she said, "Tiffany turned out okay, too."

"Of course, I'm sure. Looking forward to meeting her." He waved to the waitress. "Are you ready to order?"

"Oops, you go ahead. I haven't even looked." She scooped up one of the menus and ran her finger down the fish specials while David ordered.

When the waitress turned her attention toward Jessica, she ordered a platter with the fish of the day and a glass of pinot grigio.

The waitress asked David, "Something to drink, sir?"

"Water is fine." He gave Jessica a tight smile when the waitress left. "I don't drink alcohol."

"Oh, that's…good." Now she felt guilty about her glass of wine. Did he not drink because he had a problem with it? Alcoholism ran in families, and both Mom and Tiffany had suffered from the disease. As far as she could remember, David's biological father was a hard-drinking navy seaman. Maybe that's why David was dry.

When her wine came, she took tiny sips to make it last so she wouldn't need to order another. She still had to drive home, anyway.

They exchanged life stories over dinner, and Jessica couldn't shake the feeling that David's recitation was memorized and rather sterile. Was he trying to present a picture of perfection? She didn't need perfection from her brother, just a human connection, which she hadn't felt yet.

When David finished another story about the lessons he taught, not the kids, just the lessons, Jessica excused herself to use the ladies' room. She dismissed her disappointment. They were strangers, hadn't seen each other in over twenty-five years. The last time she'd seen David, he was barely a toddler. How would he even remember anything about her?

Maybe they wouldn't be best buds, but she had a sibling and she'd try to forge a relationship with him.

By the time she returned to the table, David had paid their bill. "I think we should get out of here while it's still light outside. I have a great idea."

"Oh?" Jessica sat down and finished her wine. She'd need it to spend any more time with David. "What do you have in mind?"

"A surprise." He clapped his hands together like a child.

"Maybe another time, David, and I hope there is another time, but you need to catch the ferry back to Edmonds and I need to drive back up the peninsula."

"You should probably wait to drive, anyway, Jessica, after drinking that wine." He tapped her glass. "I have something in mind that I think will bring us a little closer. You feel it, too, right? That bond between us is missing, but I think this little road trip will give it a boost. What do you think?"

So, he'd felt it, too. Maybe it was her fault. And when she looked into his brown eyes, so similar to Tiffany's, she decided she couldn't refuse her little brother anything.

She grabbed her purse and said, "Why not? Let's go make some new memories."

FRANTIC, HIS FINGERS SHAKING, Finn searched his computer for Celine Jerome's information. This couldn't be happening. It was all some weird mistake.

He'd questioned Wilder, and Jessica's boss admitted the DNA could be from any close male relative, even her father. Finn dug his fingers into his hair. That wouldn't work. Jessica and Tiffany had different fathers. The sample DNA from the red fiber wouldn't have matched Tiffany's DNA if it belonged to Jessica's father.

He finally found Celine's phone number and called her. "Celine Jerome, private investigations."

"Celine, you don't know me, but I'm friends with Jessica Eller. She told me all about how you located her half brother for her."

"Whatever you say. Can't discuss my work."

Finn rubbed his eyes. "I understand that, I do, but this is a matter of life and death—Jessica's. She could be in danger from her brother."

Celine sucked in a breath. "What are you talking about? He's a nice, normal guy. An army veteran, an accountant, a student."

"Would a nice, normal guy have his DNA at a murder scene? Please, Celine. I need to know his name. Jessica called him David, but I need to know his last name. Jessica is with him now and is in danger."

"Wait a minute. Who said his name was David?"

"Jessica. She told me he didn't want to give her his last name, but he said his name was David, same as it was when he was a baby."

"That may have been his name as a baby and maybe he decided to give that name to Jessica, but that's not his legal name."

"What is his legal name?"

Celine hissed on the other end of the line.

"I'll turn this over to the police, anyway, Celine, and they'll make you give up this information—only it might be too late for Jessica."

"Oh, all right, but you didn't hear it from me. His legal name is Dermott Webb."

After the call, Finn sat stunned, the phone still held to his ear. His student Dermott Webb was the Kitsap Killer? Jessica's half brother. Of course, it made sense. He was on campus. He worked in that accounting office where those women had taken the register money. Wasn't the sheriff's department supposed to be questioning and investigating anyone who'd worked with the women?

He'd call the police, but he wasn't going to waste any more time. At least he knew that Jessica and Dermott were at a restaurant in Kingston. What was the name of it? Salty Ladies? Salty Girls?

If they were meeting for dinner, they could still be there. At least it was a public place. He grabbed his keys and ran from his house. As he sped down the 104, he got Detective Morse's voicemail. He told him about the DNA, advised that he call Wilder for a better explanation, and let the detective know that he was on his way to Kingston to interrupt Jessica's dinner with her brother—the Kitsap Killer.

He made it down to Kingston in record time and asked his phone for directions to the Salty Girls restaurant. Turns out he was just two blocks away, and he swung an illegal U-turn in the middle of the street to find it.

As he passed the full parking lot, he released a sigh of relief when he spotted Jessica's car. Thank God they were still here. He'd decided not to rush in with guns blazing, accusing Dermott of being the Kitsap Killer. He'd make up some other excuse for being there…and then what? It was going to be awkward that his student, Dermott Webb, was sitting with Jessica, his sister. The sister he'd never contacted while in Fairwood. Hell, Dermott had even met Jessica once. The first time she sought him out, Dermott had been in the lecture hall.

He parked in the red zone two doors down from the restaurant and burst inside. He must've looked like a madman, as several diners turned to stare at him. His gaze darted around the room, but he didn't see them.

A hostess approached him. "Are you looking for your party, sir?"

"Yes, yeah. A couple, a tall blond woman and a man— average height, short, brown hair, maybe wearing glasses." He put out his hand about chin height. "Tall woman, wavy blond hair."

A waitress passing with two empty wineglasses slowed her gait. "I remember them. They sat at my station. The dude paid the check when the woman went to the ladies' and he stiffed me on the tip—not even ten percent. It's like he just rounded up, and I'm like, dude, this isn't Europe. He gave me a dirty look."

"Where are they?" Finn turned in a circle, hoping he'd just missed them the first time.

She shrugged. "They got out of here after he left me that crappy tip."

"Left? Her car's still here."

"Yeah, I don't know. They walked out together." She swept past him to the bar while Finn felt like screaming.

Where did they go? Why would she go anywhere with him in a place not home to either of them? Maybe something happened to her car, and he offered to drive her back to Fairwood. It wasn't that far.

He rushed from the restaurant and jogged to Jessica's car in the parking lot. He checked the tires, tried the door, peered into the windows. Everything looked normal—but nothing was normal.

He went back to his own car and sat in the front seat, gripping his steering wheel. Where could they be? How did he get her out of that restaurant? Dessert? Ice cream somewhere? Murder?

His fingers closed around his phone in his jacket pocket. He had to do it. He'd grovel, if necessary. He cupped his phone in one hand and tapped the number for the Washington State Penitentiary.

"I need to speak to prisoner 562334, Avery Plank."

Fifteen minutes later after some explanations and name-dropping, Plank came on the line. "My biographer. What can I do for you, Professor?"

"I need your…criminal mind."

Plank responded. "It's all yours. Did Miss Jessica figure out why the Kitsap Killer wants to reward her?"

"We've moved way beyond that. The Kitsap Killer is Jessica's half brother. He took her somewhere, and I don't know where. Where would he take her? Where would he want to kill her?"

Plank gave a low hum. "Really, Professor. Perhaps you're not the one to write my story. This is an obvious one. He'd want to take her to where their story began. Where he was forged in hate and resentment and envy. Where he still lives every day of his life."

Finn ended the call, cutting off Plank without a thank-you. Of course. How could he be so dense? Dermott was taking Jessica to the family home, and it wasn't far from here. He could be there within a half an hour—but would he find Jessica dead or alive?

JESSICA CLENCHED HER hands in her lap as David drove them toward the Bangor Trident Submarine Base on the other side of the peninsula. The drive took about twenty minutes, but as the miles passed, Jessica felt as if she was going back in time—to a very bad place.

A navy buddy of Jessica's grandfather had allowed Mom to live in his house north of the base with her children almost for free. The man had never checked on the property—or Mom. He'd moved to Hawaii when he retired from the service and had owed Tammy's father a big favor from their time in the navy. The house was his payback.

She'd taken Finn there once after Tiffany's murder. The place gave her the creeps, and she'd never been back. But it had been hard to refuse David.

He wanted to see the last place he'd been with his sisters and bio mom. He knew where it was. Maybe that's why he had suggested Kingston in the first place. He already had this plan in mind when he agreed to meet her.

"We're getting close, aren't we?" David flexed his fingers on the steering wheel.

"I hope you're not expecting too much, David. The last time I was there, the house was a ramshackle mess. It's probably even worse now, or maybe the owner sold it, and a new family is living there."

He lifted his shoulders. "That doesn't matter. I just want to see it. Maybe if you tell me about our family while we're there, it will mean more, give us that bond."

She lifted one side of her mouth in a weak smile. Maybe

over time, she and David could form some sort of sibling connection, but that immediate spark between them hadn't materialized.

She didn't blame him. She and Tiffany had been so close, she'd expected the same from a brother, but she and David had never even met before today, despite that first impression. When he first spoke, his voice struck a chord of familiarity in her psyche.

"This is the way, correct?" He'd slowed down where a smaller road branched off the main one on the way to Lofall.

"That's it." Jessica tugged her jacket closer around her body. Once David saw the place, he'd understand that it didn't hold good memories for her—not the kind of memories she'd want to share with a long-lost brother.

As they headed down the road, darkness closed in on them from the looming trees. His headlights picked out a few other properties on the edge of town, tucked away from the bay and the sparkling homes that inhabited its shores. This area was definitely the bad side of town, the "waterfront" a dirty creek, the people here recluses or meth heads or both.

She gave a nervous laugh. "Not much to look at."

"That doesn't matter to me. A person has to see his roots, don't you think?"

"I suppose." She jabbed a finger at the windshield as a dark, hulking structure came into view. "That's it. The old homestead."

He wheeled the car into the dirt driveway in front of the house, the headlights shining a glaring spotlight on all its misery. The front windows, both broken, stared balefully at anyone who approached. The porch sagged, a booby trap for anyone who dared to darken the door. The screen door hung from one hinge, and in the wind, must emit a fearsome squeal further warning off strangers.

"Looks like he never sold it—or did anything to repair it." She turned to him, suddenly afraid to get out of the car. "It's a mess. No place to reminisce. Let's head into town here and get some dessert. I'll tell you all about Mom and Tiffany there."

But he'd already cut the engine and had his fingers on the door handle. "Humor me, Jessica. I remember a creek out back."

Before she could continue to reason with him, he scrambled from the car, leaving the door open in his haste. As she watched him slog through the weeds in the front to reach the dirty trickle of water that ran behind the property, Jessica unclicked her seat belt.

How could he possibly remember the creek? He'd been younger than two when he left. Had he been out here by himself before?

As she twisted in her seat, the dome light illuminated a gray backpack tossed onto the back seat. The corner of what looked like a knit cap was caught in the zipper. Was it red?

"C'mon, Jessica. I found the creek and the picnic table."

The picnic table. A sour taste flooded her mouth as she remembered hiding beneath the rotting wood of the picnic table as Tiffany told one of the enraged stepdaddies that Jessica had run into the woods to avoid the strap. She gagged recalling the sound of that strap as it connected with Tiffany's bare legs.

"Jessssica!"

David's singsong voice brought her back to reality, and

she staggered out of the car and followed his trail through the tall weeds.

She rounded the house and found him standing next to the creek, which had widened since she'd last seen it. "This is it, David. Not much of anything to see, and...honestly, this place doesn't hold very fond memories for me."

"Really?" He cocked his head. "You grew up with your mother and your sister."

This place had animated her brother. Even his posture seemed different—more erect, more vital, more...aggressive.

"My mother, who had issues, my sister and a series of nasty, abusive men."

"Was my father one of those nasty, abusive men?"

"I-I don't really remember him. Navy man, didn't stick around long. None of them did." She didn't want to tell David she'd remembered his father as a violent drunk.

"I didn't stick around long. Somebody ratted out Tammy."

Her head jerked up. "Ratted out? I mean, I guess so. She couldn't care for you. It was for the best."

"Best for whom? You and Tiffany? You got all Tammy's attention, and she sent me away."

Jessica's fingertips began to buzz. This felt off. Why had David's demeanor changed? He couldn't possibly believe the things he was saying.

"Believe me, David. You were the lucky one. You got a loving, adoptive family while Tiffany and I had to deal with all of Mom's problems."

Then he laughed, a high-pitched cackle that she'd heard before, and the blood in her veins turned ice cold.

Chapter Nineteen

Finn tore down the road toward Lofall. The house sat in the forest, down a small lane that wound off the main road. There weren't that many of those. If he started seeing signs for the base, he'd gone too far.

Unless someone had bought the property and torn down the house and rebuilt, he'd remember it. Most of the houses out this way had seen better days, but Jessica's childhood home was the most dilapidated of the lot. He remembered a creek running behind it and a crumbling picnic table.

He cut his lights first. He couldn't go revving up to them, showing his hand. Also, as soon as he and Webb saw each other, the jig would be up. Maybe Webb didn't intend to harm Jessica. Finn had to make sure she got out alive. Tiffany had made that happen the first time, and he was here to finish Tiffany's work.

He rolled past one house, a glow of lights in the windows and shadows of people in the kitchen. Jessica's house had sat farther back from the road.

Then he saw it up ahead—Dermott Webb's white car. He'd seen it before on campus. Dermott had been leaving one day, getting into his car, when he spotted Finn and waved him over to ask him more questions about class.

Finn had been annoyed at the time, but now that moment had served its purpose.

Finn turned off his engine and let his car roll downhill for several feet on silent as he steered it off the road. He clicked his door closed and crept toward Dermott's car. He'd left the driver's-side door open. What did that mean? Had Jessica jumped from the car, and he'd exited in a hurry to go after her? Did Jessica even know what she was dealing with here?

She must know. She'd met Dermott in the lecture hall. She must've been shocked to see him and worried when she realized he'd given her a different name.

Then he remembered—she hadn't met Dermott. She'd been on the stage. The lights in the hall had already been dimmed. Finn knew from experience you couldn't really make out faces from the stage when the lights were low. That bit of knowledge made his breath come a little easier as he veered into the woods before he got to the decrepit house. He couldn't go charging into the middle of their meeting.

He drew his piece from his pocket. But he could end that meeting if need be.

JESSICA CLUTCHED HER throat as David pointed her own gun at her.

"Oh, it's the laugh, isn't it?" He shrugged but the gun never wavered. "You were going to find out one way or the other, weren't you?"

She fought off the fog in her brain. She had to stay alert, look for a way out. "Is the red scarf in your backpack in the car?"

"Oh, you saw that, too?" He clicked his tongue. "Now *that* was a mistake, but you should've run then, Jessica. While you had the chance."

"I-I wasn't sure what it was, and then you mentioned that damned picnic table. You have no idea what you escaped, David. No idea what the *rat* saved you from."

"That rat was Tiffany." His dark eyes narrowed, and they looked nothing like Tiffany's beautiful, soft doe eyes. "I found out a lot from my stupid adoptive mother. She told me it was the older girl who had reported Tammy to child protective services. *She* was the one who wanted me gone."

Jessica swallowed. How could he get it all wrong? "If Tiffany reported our living conditions, she was trying to save you, just like she saved me. Tiffany loved you. She tried to find you."

"She found me." His flat, cold voice chilled her to the bone.

"You met Tiffany?"

"Of course I met Tiffany. I killed Tiffany. She'd turned out just like Tammy. Sex worker." He spit into the dirt. "She was a whore, just like dear old mommy dearest."

Jessica had known the truth even before he told her, but hearing the words made her double over and sob into her hands. Lifting her head, she wiped her eyes. "I hate you."

"Yeah, yeah, I'm sure you do. You disappointed me, Jessica. You turned out normal. I was trying to get you brownie points at work, and then you betrayed me at the Gabby murder. You called the cops on me."

She dashed the tears from her cheeks. "Why here? Why now? Why those young women? Why did you pick them?"

"That's easy. My first kill was here. Tiffany was my first…and Morgan was not my second. Why those girls? Because I knew all of them from my work in the accounting office. They worked on campus. Every one of them had brought the cash bags down to the accounting office at some point. They knew me. They didn't fear me. Would you fear a guy named Dermott?"

"How did you get away with the other murders between Tiffany and Morgan? Unless—you didn't commit them in the Pacific Northwest?"

"Europe and Asia. I was stationed at various bases over the years in the army. I'm an accountant. I'm meticulous. Never got caught. Nobody ever suspected."

Jessica pressed her hands to her stomach, her gaze flickering over David's shoulder. She caught her breath when she saw a light in the woods that bordered the creek. She looked away quickly, not wanting David to notice her attention. Was someone out there? Was some stranger listening to this madman, ready to jump in and help her?

"*You* didn't suspect me. All the time wondering who killed Tiffany while seeking that killer, inviting him into your life." His grip on the gun had grown slack as he recounted his feats, but now he held it more firmly and trained it on her once again.

She wanted to give him the opportunity to brag—prolonging her life. "What about Ashley? Why did you kill her?"

He sighed, as if Ashley's murder was a huge inconvenience. "She recognized me from before. Of course, I always knew I was taking that chance by returning to the scene of my first kill, but nobody had met me here. She saw me and Tiffany together once or twice, peeked out the window when I came to get Tiffany. Nosy cow. Then we locked eyes in a coffee house yesterday, and I knew. She knew, too."

Kicking at the rotting wood on the picnic table, he said, "She ruined my aesthetic. I didn't want to kill her as the

Kitsap Killer, so I beat her with the butt of your gun. Kind of poetic, don't you think?"

"Kind of sick," Jessica growled, more angry than sad now. "Why did you start? Why did you kill our sister? She would've done anything for you."

"I told you that already." He rolled his eyes, clearly tired of explaining himself. "She's the one who ripped me away from my mother."

"You said it yourself. Tammy was no mother of the year."

"That doesn't matter," he shouted. "You and Tiffany had a family. I had adoptive strangers who never treated me like they treated their own."

A branch at the edge of the clearing shook, and Jessica marshaled all her strength not to react when she saw Finn in the bushes, his finger to his lips. How had he known she was here? In danger?

"What now, Wavy Davy?"

David's mouth dropped open, and the whites of his eyes gleamed in the dark. "What is that? Why'd you call me that?"

She spread her hands in front of her. "It's what I used to call you when you were a baby, both Tiffany and I, but I think I came up with it. I called you Davy, and when you learned how to wave, I called you Wavy Davy. You loved it. It sent you into a fit of giggles."

He choked. "You're lying."

"You know I'm not, Davy." She took a step forward, holding out her hand. "We loved you, Tiffany and I. She was the best big sister anyone could wish for. She protected me by taking on the abuse herself, and she protected you by sending you away. Mom couldn't care for a toddler. You'd barely survived your infancy and only because of Tiffany."

"She was bad. She turned out bad." The gun wavered in his hand.

"You met her. She wasn't bad. She made bad choices, but she'd changed. She loved you, and she loved me. She would've done anything to help you…and so will I. I'll do what I can to help you, Davy. Drop that gun. We can walk away from this together."

His head sank and a sob escaped his lips. That's when Finn made a move, waving his arm over his head. She didn't need him to spell it out for her.

As Finn shouted Dermott's name, Jessica lunged behind the picnic table, rolling beneath it, just as she used to do when she was a child.

A shot rang out, and her nostrils twitched at the smell of gunpowder. On her knees beneath the table, she peered through the legs. Both men were grappling on the ground, so she scrambled from her hiding place. She didn't want anyone to die.

By the time she was on her feet, Finn had taken her weapon from David and tossed it toward the water's edge. He had one knee on David's chest and the other on his wrist.

"Grab my phone from my pocket, Jessica, and call 911. I alerted the sheriff's department on my way out here, so someone should be close."

She leaned over the bodies and slipped Finn's phone from his pocket, meeting David's red-rimmed eyes.

As she called in the emergency, Finn leveled his gun at David's head. "Stay on the ground where you are. It's over, Dermott."

"It was over a long time ago, Professor Karlsson. It was over the day my mother gave me away."

Epilogue

Jessica stretched her wiggling toes toward the bay as she reclined on a chaise longue on Finn's deck, scratching Bodhi behind the ear. "I'm just glad I didn't put my career in jeopardy by tainting the DNA sample."

Finn walked barefoot onto the deck and handed her a glass of wine before nudging Bodhi out of the chair next to Jessica. "I don't understand why the initial test didn't show that the DNA on the red fiber was male DNA. That would've ruled you out immediately."

"Remember, it was just a trace, and they didn't know if they had enough of it to run a full test. There are different types of DNA tests, and that initial one they ran wasn't the mtDNA test for mitochondrial. That showed up in the subsequent test."

"I'm glad they didn't stop the testing. When I knew that DNA belonged to your brother and that you had just gone out to meet him that day, I went into panic mode." He reached over and ran his hand down her arm, giving her goose bumps. "I didn't want to lose you so soon after rediscovering you."

"If that's your panic mode, your focused mode must be intense. You had it together enough to contact Celine and to remember the name of the restaurant where I was meeting David... Dermott." She slid her hand in his, lacing her fingers with his. "How did you know where to find us? You never told me that. I know I took you there once, but how did you figure out we'd be at the house?"

"I have a confession to make." He swirled the beer in his bottle and took a sip as he squinted at the sun dipping into the bay. "I contacted an expert."

"An expert?" She hung her leg over the side of the chaise and ran her foot over the soft fur on Bodhi's back.

"I called Avery Plank." He squeezed her hand. "And I don't regret it. He pointed out the obvious, but I wasn't thinking straight. When he said Dermott would go back to the beginning, where it all started for him, I knew he'd take you to the house. And why not? Nobody suspected your brother yet. Why would anyone think the Kitsap Killer would take you to your childhood home?"

She wrinkled her nose. "Ugh, Plank must've reveled in that."

"I didn't give him a chance, but I'm sure he'll remind me at our next meeting."

Finn asked, "Are you going to visit Dermott in prison? At least he confessed to all the slayings, and he's working with the authorities in Europe and Asia to solve some of those cases."

Disentangling her fingers from his, Jessica put her feet on the deck and stroked Bodhi's back. There was a reason people used dogs for therapy. Petting Bodhi calmed her nerves enough to answer. "I don't know if I can ever forgive him for taking Tiffany from me and killing all those other women. It makes me ill to think we have the same mother."

"But different fathers. Sounds like Dermott's bio dad was a piece of work. Sometimes nature is stronger than nurture."

She rubbed her tingling nose. "I'm not sure his adoptive family was all that nurturing."

Finn snorted. "If you believe Dermott. He's just like Plank, blaming everything on his upbringing for sympathy and understanding."

She glanced up, her hand still on Bodhi's back. "You're still writing the book, even though your link to Plank, finding Tiffany's body, has been blown out of the water?"

"That was an important hook, for sure. That's how I got my agent interested in the book, but I've got an even better hook now—how I saved Tiffany's sister from the Kitsap Killer who let Plank confess to his crime." He laced his fingers together. "The stories are linked. My agent is happy—if you can be happy about murder."

She drilled a knuckle into his biceps. "Oh, is *that* why you're dating me?

"Dating?" He placed his bottle on the deck and shifted his chair to face her. "Is that all we're doing?"

A smile played over her lips. "Well, we keep getting interrupted. I think we're destined to circle the flame."

"Come over here." Leaning forward, he lightly clasped her wrists and tugged her toward him. "I think I'm ready to jump into the fire."

She stepped over Bodhi, who barely lifted his head, and sat in Finn's lap, her legs swinging over the side of his chair. As he pulled her close and kissed her mouth, she felt that spark she'd always felt for him. But this time there was nothing between them.

She murmured against his lips. "Let the inferno begin."

* * * * *